MURDER IN
THE VATICAN

by

Eugene L. Mendonsa, Ph.D.

©2016

This book is dedicated to all who have suffered at the hands of true believers.

Most of the characters in this book are purely fictional. Any similarities between them and real individuals are purely coincidental. Those who were real characters have been manipulated by the author and given fictional actions and words.

MURDER IN THE VATICAN

CHAPTER ONE

The Vatican is a dagger in the heart of Italy.
  – Thomas Paine

Father Nathan Mendelsohn had developed himself into a scholar of the history of the Catholic Church. He had completed his Bachelor of Arts degree at Notre Dame University in Indiana, a Masters at Loyola in Chicago and a Ph.D in Biblical history at Oxford University in England.

It was his first book that drew him to the attention of the Pope, Martin VI. It had the provocative title of *Crimes of the Early Popes.* It surprised many in the church that Pope Martin would even read a book like that, let alone invite the author to the Vatican for a job interview.

The Vatican City State (*Stato della Città del Vaticano*) was a walled municipality within the city of Rome. Despite its medieval structure and culture, it was the smallest internationally recognized independent state in the world, with less than a thousand residents in an area smaller than many farms in America.

The Bishop of Rome – the Pope – ruled this ecclesiastical or sacerdotal-monarchical state with deified authority. With the Pope were the topmost state officers, who were all high-ranking Catholic clergy.

The unique economy of the Vatican City State was supported financially by the sale of tourist souvenirs, postage stamps, admission fees to museums, the sale of church publications and investments.

The Vatican City State was distinct from the *Sancta Sedes* or Holy See. The latter was the Catholic Church administration, an ecclesiastical

jurisdiction of the worldwide church and the Episcopal See of the Pope.

In 1929 Pope Pius XI signed the Lateran Treaty with Prime Minister Benito Mussolini in what some have seen as a pact with the devil. *Il Papa* promised to support the Fascist State of Mussolini in return for sovereignty for the Vatican City State. He was also prohibited by the treaty from becoming involved in Italian politics, or from criticizing Italian military aggression.

Under Pius XII the Vatican City followed a policy of neutrality even though Rome was occupied by the Germans in 1943 and a year later by the Allies. In neither case was Vatican City conquered.

MURDER IN THE VATICAN

In 1939, on the eve of war, Pious II had assiduously tried to mediate between Hitler and Mussolini on the one hand and the Allies on the other. He failed to bring a halt to the march to war.

Father Mendelsohn arrived at the Catholic enclave in the Eternal City, the ancient city of the Roman Emperors. On a cheerful spring day Father Mendelsohn stepped from the taxi with some weary stiffness to his step, but with a heart filled with axious anticipation at being in the home of *i Papi*, the 266 Popes that had proceeded the present one, Pope Martin VI, *il papa*.

After landing at Leonardo da Vinci Airport the taxi carried the thirty-something *reverendo* past *Ponte Galeria*, alongside the *Fiume Tevere*, past the Roman Colosseum to the *Piazza San*

MURDER IN THE VATICAN

Pietro and the famous Saint Peter's Basilica.

The *portiere* was there to meet him and carried his two light bags past St. Peter's Tomb and the Sistine Chapel into the *Cortile del Belvedere* where the trailing Father caught his first view of the Vatican Library where he would be spending much of his time.

Being small, the Vatican had always had an active rumor mill, which was quite vigorous and it went into full gear divining reasons for the arrival of Father Mendelsohn, a junior priest and an obvious outsider.

The most accepted explanation was that the 87-year-old Pope was getting senile. In reality, in spite of a failing body, *il Papa* was mentally very sharp and had an honorable and important role for Father Mendelsohn to play at the Vatican.

Pope Martin was a modern Pontiff, even though he was Italian and came from a prominent family in Milan, one that had provided the Vatican with more than a few Popes in the past. As a young man, before he decided to become a priest, Martin had been educated, uncharacteristically, outside of Italy at Cambridge University in England, where he was, appropriately, a member of Jesus College. It is perhaps because of that secular training that he was considered a "progressive" Pope.

Pope Martin not only read *Crimes of the Early Popes*, but he enjoyed the book, especially the detailed scholarship apparent on its 789 pages. Published by Cambridge University Press, *Crimes of the Early Popes* did not make the *New*

MURDER IN THE VATICAN

York Times Best Seller List, but it was warmly received by those academics who followed church history.

The Pope's secretary, Monsignor Alfio Corvi, led Father Mendelsohn along the parquet floored entry hall flanked on both sides by the busts of departed Popes and into the Pontiff's private chambers and seated him in an easy chair. There he sat for twenty minutes awaiting the arrival of *il Papa*, but he had a lot to look at, being in the Room of Heliodorus frescoed by Raphael. Through the high ceiling windows shone the warm Italian sun that bathed the Apostolic Palace.

When the Pope did arrive he was being helped by Monsignor Corvi, as he seemed frail, even gaunt and strain showed in his eyes and along the tight lines of his face. A thin long-boned man

MURDER IN THE VATICAN

who definitely looked Italian with a
dusky complexion and a hooked nose,
Pope Martin's real name was Taavetti
Bellomi di Pasqua.

His Eminence was wearing the
traditional skullcap and a white gown
that hung to the floor. Entering the
room he gave the impression of an
arriving angel. Around his neck he wore
a long chain supporting the Pope's
Pectoral Cross, which showed an image
of the crucified Christ against a
background of sheep. Above the flock
was a white descending dove.

The thing that Father Mendelsohn
noticed most about the Pope were his
hands. The Papal ring seemed
monstrously large on skin and bones,
hands that looked like they had died and
were waiting for the rest of the body to
catch up.

MURDER IN THE VATICAN

Once seated in a high-backed chair and introductions were out of the way, Pope Martin explained, "My son, I have invited you to the Holy See for a very important mission. As you know, I have read your fine book and have come to know that you are aware of the misdeeds of some Popes in the past."

"Holy Father, it was not only the Popes who were breaking the rules. There were many others in the Vatican that deviated from God's law."

"Yes, yes and that's exactly what I want to talk about. While I have tried in my years as Pope to adhere as closely to God's dictates as I could, there have been others around me that have walked others paths, so to speak."

"I am also aware of the problems of the present, Holy Father."

MURDER IN THE VATICAN

"So that we can be on the same page, please tell me what you have seen from the outside and then I will tell you what I have experienced by living and working within these walls." The Pope made a sweeping gesture with his cadaverous right hand, on it the Papal Ring of the Fisherman seemed out of place.

Father Mendelsohn shifted somewhat uneasily in his chair. "Well sir, it would seem that the Vatican Bank has been corrupted and is being used to launder Mafia funds among others."

The Vatican Bank was short for the *Istituto per le Opere di Religione* (IOR), but it was not an ordinary bank because it had immunities and privileges that derived from its presumed religious nature.

MURDER IN THE VATICAN

The IOR performed functions similar to that of a secular bank, but unlike a normal bank, the Vatican Bank did not loan money and its accounts did not collect interest; nor did it make a profit for shareholders or owners. Instead, the IOR acted as a clearinghouse for Vatican accounts, moving funds received from various sources to destinations within the wider church.

Father Mendelsohn continued, "I think the bank directors are corrupt and are in cahoots with some very un-Christian characters beyond these walls."

"Yes," said the Pope, "I am aware of that problem, perhaps our number one problem. But there are others, are there not?"

MURDER IN THE VATICAN

"Yes, Your Eminence. Conceivably number two is the political riff between you and some very conservative Bishops."

"Do you know these Bishops?"

"Only by name and reputation."

"And who do you think my number one political opponent is among them?"

"Well, I don't know if he is the number one adversary, but it would appear to me that Cardinal Donati is very near the top of the list."

"Yes, I agree that Giovani Donati sits on the other side of the isle, so to speak."

Father Mendelsohn continued, "There may be other minor problems, but these two seem to be the greatest challenges for Your Holiness and of course they may well be intertwined."

MURDER IN THE VATICAN

"As you can see I am very old and not all that well. I will soon meet our maker and I would like these problems dealt with before I leave this mortal frame and that is why I have brought you to the Holy See."

"I am at your service, Holy Father."

"I am sick with crime, my son. I need you to investigate the behavior of such men as Cardinal Giovani Donati. I know there are bad things being done in the name of religion and this is surely the work of Satan. But before I can act I need hard evidence to take before the Council of Cardinals."

Father Mendelsohn answered, "As I said Your Holiness, I am at your service. How would you like me to proceed?"

MURDER IN THE VATICAN

"I have replaced you in your pastoral calling in St. Mary's Church in California. You will be shown to your apartment here in Vatican City. I have equipped it with all the latest computer equipment and you will have complete access to the *Bibliotheca Apostolica Vaticana*. As you speak and read Italian I know that you know that to be the Vatican Apostolic Library."

"Yes sir, I am aware of it. I used it in writing *Crimes of the Early Popes*, but accessed it online mostly."

"And I suppose that you are also aware that it is one of the oldest libraries on earth and contains one of the most noteworthy collections of historical texts. It currently has 75,000 codices from throughout history, in addition to 1.1 million printed books, which include some 8,500 *incunabula*, those most rare of early books and manuscripts."

"Again Your Eminence, I have consulted some of them and I am familiar with the library's immense collections. You have set me a daunting task."

"And a dangerous one. Before you accept this apostolic calling father, you must understand that these men are in and of themselves violent, but they are also in association with others who do not hesitate to assassinate those who get in their way."

"The Mafia."

"Precisely, the Sons of Satan."

"I am in the hands of God Your Holiness. I am aware of the treachery of these men and I accept the calling."

"Then you may begin as soon as you get settled into your new rooms.

MURDER IN THE VATICAN

Please be on guard at all times. They will know that you are here and why."

Father Mendelsohn made the sign of the cross and said, "I have a special protector in our lord and savior."

Pope Martin said, "*Andare con Dio*," as he made the Apostolic Sign of Benediction with his raised skeletal hand. To Father Mendelsohn it looked as if it was going to crack and fall to pieces with the motion.

MURDER IN THE VATICAN

CHAPTER TWO

The belief in a supernatural source of evil is not necessary; men alone are quite capable of every wickedness.
– Joseph Conrad

Cardinal Giovani Donati, the leader of Vatican conservatives and head of the Vatican's financial supervisory body, the AIF or *Autorità di Informazione Finanziaria*, called an emergency meeting. Many of the Bishops were vacationing at luxury resorts throughout Europe and the Caribbean and one was in Dubai as a guest of the Emir.

They were not especially happy at being called back to Vatican City on short notice in August, the time when Europeans generally take their extended

vacations, but when Donati told them
the reason each one hurried back to
Rome as fast as they could manage.

Donati was fat by anybody's
standards, though he thought of himself
simply as a big man in two senses of the
word. With a baldhead, pursed lips, a
pig-like nose, blond eyebrows and
sallow skin he looked to many like a
Yorkshire Pig _aka_ The Large White.

When they were all assembled in
the AIF salon Donati began, "You have
all probably heard of that smear book
Crimes of the Early Popes. Pope Martin
has brought this author, Father Nathan
Mendelsohn, to the Vatican and installed
him in an apartment."

"That can only mean one thing,"
said Bishop Cosimo Rossi, a Prelate who
was perhaps even more conservative
than Donati. "The fucking Pope is going

to get him poking his nose where it shouldn't be poked."

"I suggest that we poke back," said Cardinal Giovani Donati.

The Bishops had taken the precaution to have the room swept for bugs prior to opening their meeting and felt free to speak openly, at least till the next assembly when it would have to be swept again.

Cardinal Donati was a big man for an Italian and when he wore his ecclesiastical garments he was an impressive figure, a man who commanded attention by his very presence. He favored the black gown, red cape, red skullcap and red sash.

The much smaller and less impressive Bishop Rossi asked a rhetorical question, "Do we use Servio again?" He was referring to the top man in the Roman Mafia, *Don* Servio Ganza.

Whenever this small band of Bishops needed some dirty work done – what the CIA called "wet work" – they summoned Ganza whose power in Rome was legendary.

The *Don* could have a man killed with a simple phone call or the flick of his wrist. In fact, he was well known for this gesture, which could not be picked up by any listening devises planted by the Italian police, the *Arma dei Carabinieri*, or the *Mafia Italiana della Compito Unità* – the Italian Mafia Task Force. With a turn of his wrist his gunsels knew that the individual in question should not draw too many more breaths.

"But of course," was Donati's simple reply. "When we need him the

MURDER IN THE VATICAN

Don, being a good Catholic and a good
Italian, is always there."
****

Don Servio Ganza looked like a
Mafia boss with his broad peasant face
and his thick chevron mustache over
pouty lips. But after meeting him for the
first time folks remembered his bullet
eyes that seemed so dark that they
almost made his olive skin seem white.

Ganza was seated at his usual
table in his favorite *ristorante*, the well-
known *Rinfresco a Domicilio Roma*. He
had a cigarette dangling from his thick
lips and a glass of Campari in his cruel
hands. The veins were so prominent
that Ganza's hands appeared to have
blood on them.

There were also two gunsels at
the green colored door and one on
either side of the head of the Roman

MURDER IN THE VATICAN

Mafia. These were the men who would kill with the flick of the boss's wrist.

When Cardinal Giovani Donati entered the restaurant he was frisked by the goons at the door, in spite of his elevated status at the Vatican.

Don Ganza did not rise to greet Donati, but simply motioned for him to sit.

"*Vino*?" asked Ganza, digging at the cardinal, who always drank cognac.

The Bishop, who was a heavy drinker, shook his head irritably. "Cognac."

The waiter who was hovering at the table quickly disappeared and within a minute was pouring Cognac Frapin into a $163 Spiegelau XL glass. When the Bishop held the glass in his hand he was holding over $250. He

liked visiting the Mafia head, even if he
was often irritated by his cousin.

"So what brings you out of your
medieval cocoon?" asked Ganza, poking
the Cardinal maliciously. He had a mean
streak, something that helped propel
him to the top of the crime syndicate in
Rome. Donati liked what Ganza could
do for him, but not the man behind the
power.

In a tight voice Donati managed to
say, "A problem, as usual *Don* Ganza. A
small problem or a big problem, I don't
know at this point, but I wanted to make
you aware that we may need your
services again."

Somewhat disingenuously the *Don*
said, "As you already know, as a fervent
Catholic I am always on call for the
Mother Church. Can you give me some

MURDER IN THE VATICAN

details of what we may be dealing with?"

"Our senile Pope has hired a man who has written a salacious and damaging book, a scar on the Holy Church."

"Why would he do that?"

Donati downed the remainder of the pricy cognac, which most people sipped. It was a small thing, but it irked the *Don* that every time Donati showed his face he guzzled expensive drinks like they were water.

Grudgingly Ganza made the "once more" sign to the waiter and Donati continued: "I am not sure why. The Father is getting on in years and I am hoping it is just a silly fascination with the more salacious and titillating aspects of our church history, but I fear that there is a more sinister motive."

24

MURDER IN THE VATICAN

"Like what? asked Ganza, as the waiter poured more cognac. The *Don* had the Campari bottle on the table and emptied it into his glass. The waiter saw this and quickly appeared with a new bottle and took away the empty.

"Like having this Father Mendelsohn look into our affairs."

"You've been screwing those young girls again, I guess," said Ganza with a malicious smirk on his face. He knew that Donati preferred young boys.

"Not that kind of affair. The financial stuff. You know what I mean. Stop being cruel."

"Stop being so sensitive. I'm just having some fun with you." Ganza lit another Galois cigarette. He blew smoke into the silver-blue haze that hung over the tables.

MURDER IN THE VATICAN

Irritated, Donati said, "Be serious. This thing is not to be scoffed at. At least I think Mendelsohn may be here to dig for facts on our dealings and as you know there is a lot of dirt at the Vatican Bank."

Maliciously Ganza said, "I suspect that God loves sinners as well as saints and you Bishops have both options covered, don't you?"

"Unlike Mafioso," replied Donati, trying to be as mean as the *Don.* He never managed to quite pull it off.

If most men talked to the head of the Roman Mafia like Donati was doing they wouldn't live to make it out of the restaurant, but not only did these two men go way back to the playground at *La Scuola Primaria di Nostra Signora*, but they were cousins. As such, they enjoyed a joking relationship. But sometimes jokes can hurt.

Donati also knew that Ganza's fondest wish as a child was to grow up to be a strong Prime Minister of Italy like Mussolini. Being a strong leader of the Roman Mafia was the backseat of the Maserati, but Donati thought that his Mafioso cousin probably still had political aspirations. He wanted to be in the driver's seat.

"So you want us to whack this Father ... what's his name?"

"Mendelsohn. Father Nathan Mendelsohn. No, not yet. Let's see what he's up to in the Vatican. If it's just another history book, we'll leave him to it. If he starts meddling in our recent activities, that's a goat and not a sheep."

"I hear you like to fuck both."

MURDER IN THE VATICAN

"Stop it! Give me some more
cognac. I only come around for the free
drinks, not your goddamned jokes."
Donati was almost always irritated by
his interaction with his cousin, but he
was even more perturbed by the fact
that Ganza knew of his pedophilia.

"That'll be ten Our Fathers for
using the Lord's name in vain," said
Ganza. He always had to have the last
word.

MURDER IN THE VATICAN

CHAPTER THREE

What we do, we keep a secret. We are not to be seen or heard by the rest of the world.
– Mark Simo, *RKU*

In Washington DC the FBI Investigative Officer assigned to the Mafia, Jack Dennison, was sitting down with his counterpart, Marty Franks, who was assigned to look into the murky affairs of the Vatican Bank. They were in the cafeteria of the J. Edgar Hoover Building, which had a picture window looking out on Pennsylvania Avenue. It was so hot out that you could almost see the steam coming off the concrete.

Jack Dennison said, "So last time we drank this putrid coffee together you were telling me that the officialdom of Christianity in Rome has allowed for some hoodwinks in the recent past and it's equally apparent that the mischief is not finished."

"And the Mafia is involved," added Marty Franks.

"I guess that's why the Director wants us to work together."

"It would seem so, we both speak Italian and have lots of experience over there."

"So tell me what you've found so far," said Dennison.

"Well, the head of the Vatican Bank is Bishop Paul Sadowski. He is a known associate of men of questionable character, namely your guy in Rome, *Don* Servio Ganza. And then there is Franco Lombardi Lippi."

"He's the P2 guy, isn't he?"

"Yeah, *Propaganda Due.* The Masons."

MURDER IN THE VATICAN

Freemasonry has its roots in the association of craftsmen in guilds in medieval times. The Roman Catholic Church as long objected to the Masons based on the allegation that Masonry teaches a naturalistic or deistic religion that is in contradiction to Church doctrine. Several Papal pronouncements have been issued against Freemasonry. The first came from Pope Clement XII when he made his In *eminenti apostolatus* in 1738. Since then Popes have reiterated that Canon Law explicitly declares Freemasonry so heinous that Catholics found to be members of a Masonic lodge are to be automatically excommunicated.

"I thought the Vatican mucky-mucks weren't supposed to be members of P2," said Dennison.

MURDER IN THE VATICAN

"Hell, they're not even supposed to associate with Masons, but they do and there are lots of Bishops that are secret members of P2, mostly rightwing blokes."

"Your years in the London office are shining through Franks."

"Blokes, chaps, dudes or whatever – these guys are crooked as a dog's hind leg."

"So tell me more," urged Dennison. He had been staring out the window while listening to his counterpart. Half his brain was counting the limousines cruising down Pennsylvania Avenue. He was up to 14 when Franks said:

"Okay, apparently this Bishop Paul Sadowski is operating in both the world of the Vatican Bank and in its

MURDER IN THE VATICAN

counterpart in the secular world, the Amrosiano Bank.

As a Board Member of the overseas branch of Ambrosiano Bank based in Nassau Sadowski has connections to the Mafia. I don't know if it was your Roman Mafia, but definitely *La Cosa Nostra* of some sort."

"They're pretty much all the same sort – criminals," said Dennison cynically, "but in Rome, and more broadly in Italy, the term *la cosa nostra* is not used. It's an American thing."

Franks continued, "It was all about money-laundering through Sadowski's banking connections inside and out of the Vatican. The Vatican Bank under Sadowski is the major shareholder in the Ambrosiano Bank – you might say a shady shareholder."

33

MURDER IN THE VATICAN

"As I understand it the Vatican is not supposed to be involved with outside financial institutions."

Franks, who could be as cynical as Jack Dennison, said, "And they're not supposed to cornhole young altar boys either."

"Be nice. They are sanctified, don't ya know."

"Sanctified my ass," continued Franks, "Sadowski and others, such as Danilo Cavallo, head of the Ambrosiano Bank, are secret members of a P2 lodge in Rome that seems to have been intricately involved in the murky financial affairs of the Vatican."

Jack Dennison said, "We've had our eye on P2. It was actually founded by an Italian Parliamentary Commission of Inquiry and designed to be a secret criminal organization involved in money laundering for the Mafia. Maybe even ISIS or other radical groups. Can you believe it? Some government they got over there."

"When it comes to the Vatican Bank and the Italians I can believe that Satan has God locked away in solitary confinement."

"Cute," said Dennison appreciative of the joke.

"Anyway, both Sadowski and Cavallo have been linked to the mysterious and sudden death of Pope John Paul I in 1978. He only got to be the Pontiff for 33 days and he was poisoned. It's rumored that the Pontiff was about to reveal information about criminal behavior at the Vatican Bank."

"Well, Pope Martin better watch his papal hind end then."

"Yeah, especially since we have information that he has brought in the author of *Crimes of the Early Popes*."

"That's Father Mendelsohn, I believe."

"He's the one and I can only see one reason why the Pope has set him up in a flat in Vatican City."

"To do for the present what he did for the past."

"Precisely. There is far too much murkiness in the connections between P2, Ambrosiano Bank and the Vatican for a true believer like Martin VI to suffer. He's close to the end and he wants this shit cleaned up before his term is up."

"He smells smoke and wants Father Mendelsohn to find some fire."

MURDER IN THE VATICAN

"Right, so our job, according to Director Donald, is to also dig for dirt – prosecutable dirt."

"You got your shovel and I've got mine," said Jack Dennison.

Marty Franks replied almost realistically, "Jack, we may need a backhoe."

****

Franco Lombardi Lippi, the Worshipful Master of *Propaganda Due*, was dressed in his black robe with an apron displaying the symbol of his High Office – the Masonic Square and Compasses. Over his chair hung the illuminated Letter G, representing God and Geometry, both important to the members of P2, as with other types of Masons.

Lippi made the sign of the G in the air, signifying that the meeting had come

MURDER IN THE VATICAN

to an end. He waited for each member to pass by his chair and offer the secret handshake. Anyone who could not perform the handshake properly would not leave the hall alive.

When Monsignor Alfio Corvi, the Pope's secretary, offered his hand, Franco Lippi indicated that he wished to speak with him. Accordingly, Corvi moved to the side and waited until all the ritual handshaking was over, then Lippi motioned to follow him into his chambers behind the altar.

Inside and seated, the Worshipful Master said, "I got your note. What's this all about?"

"I didn't want to spell it out in writing, but it seems that the Pope has brought in an investigator to probe the workings of our financial dealings and

MURDER IN THE VATICAN

perhaps more. I really don't know the extent of his warrant."

"We have become very wealthy men through our associations with the Vatican Bank and Ambrosiano. Let's not let anyone or anything change that. You are in a prime position to monitor this for us Monsignor. I trust that you will gather as much information as you can and keep me informed."

"That is my aim, Worshipful Master."

The two Masons parted after performing the sacred handshake.

MURDER IN THE VATICAN

CHAPTER FOUR

*As long as I hold it, as long as I use it, the knife lives,
lives in order to take life, but it has to be
commanded, it has to have me to tell it to kill, and it
wants to, it wants to plunge and thrust and cut and
stab and gouge, but I have to want it to as well, my
will has to join with its will.*
– Patrick Ness, *The Knife of Never Letting Go*

Father Nathan Mendelsohn spent the first year collecting a great deal of information on the goings on at the Vatican Bank and Ambrosiano Bank. In the 12 months he discovered several things. And Donati was becoming anxious.

In the 1930s Pope Pius XI had appointed the German who had previously reorganized the *Reichsbank* for Hitler, Bernard Fertig to run the Vatican Bank. Fertig was an operative who wasconsidered to be a financial genius. He was given the window dressing of a three-Cardinal committee to oversee the handling of the money, but in fact he had complete authority and control, not them.

Furthermore, Fertig was to have free access to the Holy Father. His mission was to make the church wealthy and he did so through shrewd investments. Several of these were in manufacturing plants and companies that produced for the war machine of the Fascists in Italy and Nazis in Germany.

Furthermore, he bought up so much Italian real estate that the Vatican became the second largest landowner in the country, after the Italian State.

While the world was gripped in depression, the Catholic Church was becoming enormously wealthy. Money poured into the Vatican – so much cash that Fertig was faced with the problem of concealing the enormous holdings and vast earnings of the Catholic Church from the public eye and especially from the poor Catholics who put money in the collection basket every time they attended Mass.

The surplus revenue was now diverted from the Church's corporations into inaccessible Swiss bank accounts. Some also went into the secular Ambrosiano Bank.

The true wealth of the Catholic Church would only be known to the Pope and his trusted advisors. For everyone else the figure would remain a matter of conjecture.

Father Mendelsohn could see that Pius was not so pious, but very shrewd at squirrelling money away. With the help of Fertig. The young priest was uncovering facts that showed that secrecy in the modern Vatican allowed the officials of the Holy See to divert church funds into confidential accounts in a manner that was hidden from state inquiry, or from public awareness. Most in the Vatican knew nothing of the dirty dealings. Mendelsohn wondered, *Who knows where all this money is now that Pope Pius is dead?*

The young priest knew that the Pope and officials of the Vatican were supposed to be spiritual guides and supporters of the poor; but privately they operated in the reign of Pope Pius XI as ardent capitalists, a stance that apparently interfered with their calling as shepherds of the poor and needy. The "donation of Mussolini" helped to unbind their greed.

MURDER IN THE VATICAN

And that greed hides in the vaults of the Istituto per le Opere di Religione, thought Father Mendelsohn who came to know that the Vatican Bank was not an ordinary bank because it had immunities and privileges that derived from its presumed religious nature. It did not loan money and its accounts did not collect interest; nor did it make a profit for shareholders or owners. *But it's a perfect place to hide money.*

Father Mendelsohn was also finding out something about the culture of the Vatican. Surrounded by the modern world, the Pope, Cardinals, Bishops and other high ranking officers of the church lived in a cloister that resembled a Medieval fortress, perhaps only highlighted by the vanities of their miters and capes.

MURDER IN THE VATICAN

But he came to see the problem less in terms of architecture or costumes; but rather that the Cardinals, Archbishops And Bishops who managed the institutional church lived behind guarded walls in a pre-Enlightenment world.

Within their reserve they had remained largely untouched by the democratic revolutions in France and America.

In that cloistered milieu, church officials had come to develop a subculture in which they had taken on an air of invincibility and privilege, which in most cases could merely be seen as silly arrogance; but which, in a few cases, had led to sexual deviance by some in the church, while other ecclesiastical officers participated in concealing these crimes from the public and secular officials. Others, who saw themselves as financial geniuses, were outright thieves.

After a year of digging in files, archives and books, Father Mendelsohn decided it was time to confront some of the principal players he had identified. There was Cardinal Giovani Donati – leader of conservatives and head of the Vatican's financial supervisory body, the AIF (*Autorità di Informazione Finanziaria*).

Another operative was Bishop Paul Sadowski, head of the Vatican Bank. Father Mendelsohn had seen them together often, almost like they were joined at the hip.

Then there were the outside players – Danilo Cavallo – Head of the Ambrosiano Bank, in which the Vatican had invested Church funds. Another was the shadowy Franco Lombardi Lippi. Father Mendelsohn found it strange that Vatican officials were meeting with this man from time to time, because he was the Worshipful Master of *Propaganda Due,* a suspicious Masonic organization that was off limits to Vatican personnel. *How is he connected to the money?* wondered the priest.

Then there were the rumors that Father Mendelsohn had heard, principally linking Donati and Sadowski to the head of the Roman Mafia, Servio Ganza. The Mafia and P2 kept popping up.

Unfortunately Father Mendelsohn decided to begin his interviews with Cardinal Donati. That was a fatal mistake.

****

MURDER IN THE VATICAN

Donati agreed to see Father Mendelsohn, but he wasn't happy with the presence of the young cleric in the Vatican. He pursed his porcine lips in a grimace when he thought of the mess the Pope had created for him.

"So the Pope has set you the task of poking your nose in Vatican business, is that it?"

Quietly, Father Mendelsohn replied, "His Eminence has asked me to investigate any wrongdoing or financial malfeasance with regard to the Vatican Bank."

Bellowing, "You little shit! Do you know that I am charged with the responsibligy of making sure that isn't the case? How dare you insinuate that there is corruption at the bank?"

"I am not insinuating anything. I am doing what the Pontiff asked me to do and that is investigating and that means looking for facts and evidence, not making facile accusations."

"The very investigation is an allegation," roared the Cardinal.

"If government auditors go into to audit the Bank of Italy they are not making accusations. They are merely looking for indications of misconduct."

"The Vatican Bank is different," countered Donati.

"Yes, I am aware of that and that is precisely why I am doing my research. This is being done in the very absence of proper auditing and third party oversight that any normal bank experiences."

Donati was silent for a minute while he lit a cigarette. He sucked on it and exhaled a stream of bluish smoke that drifted up toward the high ceiling of his ancient office. "As I said, you are overlooking the fact that we have a committee of Cardinals, of which I am the head. It is tasked with doing what secular auditors do at outside banks."

"From what I have found so far, I think that is a self-serving exaggeration."

"The Cardinal jumped to his feet and slammed his fist down on the top of his desk. As he did do his cigarette dropped from his piggish lips and he sputtered incoherently as he tried to find it on the floor.

While Donati was so engaged, Father Mendelsohn also stood up and said, "It was not my intent to upset you sir. I will take my leave and wish you a good day." With that he turned and left the office.

MURDER IN THE VATICAN

On his knees Donati found his cigarette and proceeded to burn his fingers. He bellowed so loudly that his valet in the outer office joked with a nearby secretary, "I think they may have heard that in the 14th century," which the savvy valet knew was the century in which the office building had been built.

****

Father Mendelsohn was writing up some notes on his contentious interview with Cardinal Donati. It had not gone well. The Father could see that Donati was dragging his feet on every question and evading most.

Father Mendelsohn decided that he was going to have to pull an end run or two on the Cardinal by talking to his staff members.

He was just finishing his write-up when there was a knock at the door. He put on his slippers and made his way to open it. When he did he found an apparent member of the Vatican Curia at his door. He was wearing the frock of a Monsignor, but Father Mendelsohn had never seen the Prelate before.

The man seemed to be handing him a package, but instead drove an AGA Campolin 13-inch Italian Picklock Cocobolo stiletto into his stomach and pushed the priest back into his flat.

The attacker then jabbed the stiletto again into Father Mendelsohn's heart, a mortal stab.

The Mafioso then cut out his heart and stuffed it into his mouth, a typical Mafia message. *Even the fucking Pope will get this message*, thought the killer as he wiped off the knife, folded the switchblade and slipped it into his cassock pocket.

MURDER IN THE VATICAN

The Mafioso couldn't wait to get out of the damn robe. It made him feel like a girl and he didn't like the feeling. Killing the priest didn't bother him at all. *After all*, he thought, as he walked swiftly to his car, *the knife did the killing*.

MURDER IN THE VATICAN

CHAPTER TWELVE

*It often seems to me that's all detective work
is, wiping out your false starts and beginning again.
Yes, it is very true, that. And it is just what some
people will not do. They conceive a certain theory,
and everything has to fit into that theory. If one little
fact will not fit it, they throw it aside. But it is always
the facts that will not fit in that are significant.*
– Agatha Christie, *Death on the Nile*

At first Pope Martin was shocked when he heard the news of Father Mendelsohn's murder. Then he became frightened. Not for himself. He had known that he could be killed easily anytime the evil ones wanted him out of the way, but he was frightened for the Church, the organization to which he had devoted his long life.

Now he didn't know who to trust in the Vatican. He had gone outside to get Father Mendelsohn, now he had to do it again.

Pope Martin thought long and hard on the subject. *Another priest? There aren't any with those credentials. Father Mendelsohn was unique in his historical perspective on Church deviance. A secular man? But who?*

No Italian police had jurisdiction in the matter of Father Mendelsohn's murder. It was handled internally by the *Corpo della Gendarmeria dello Stato della Città del Vaticano* – the Vatican police force.

The *Gendarmeria*'s top cop was Celso Palmisano, an Italian peasant who had worked his way to the top of the police force. Of course, he came armed with a Masters Degree in Criminality from Cambridge University in England, where he went up on a scholarship, having passed every examination in Italy with high marks.

Monsignor Alfio Corvi, the Pope's private secretary, tried to convince the Pontiff that he should use Captain Palmisano to investigate the murder, but Pope Martin wanted his chosen man to do more than that. He still wanted to ferret out the corruption in the Vatican Bank and elsewhere in the structure of the Vatican.

Nonetheless, he agreed to meet with Palmisano. When he did he was pleased to find that the *Gendarmeria*'s top cop didn't quite fit the stereotype of a policeman. He found him educated, erudite and swift on the uptake. What was more, he found that Captain Palmisano didn't want the job, but he knew someone who was perfect for it.

MURDER IN THE VATICAN

"Your Holiness if you have read my dossier you know that I went to Cambridge University to study at the Institute of Police Management. It was there that I met a man who would do a good job for you. His name is Stone Harrison."

"And why do you think this Mr. Harrison would be a good fit?"

"You've described to me a task that calls for more than a detective, which of course he is; but he also holds a Ph.D in history."

"That makes him smart and persevering, but I don't see how it makes him any more qualified than yourself."

"His Ph.D dissertation was entitled, *The Evolution of the Vatican Governmental Structure.*"

MURDER IN THE VATICAN

"Oh, I see your point Captain. And where is Mr. ... excuse me, Dr. Stone."

"Dr. Harrison, Your Eminence. Stone is his given name. His father was the Earl of Jersey."

"Isn't Stone a rather odd first name?"

"With respect Your Holiness, what was the name of Saint Peter in Latin?"

"*Petrus.*"

"And the meaning of *Petrus* in English?

"Rock. I get your point. If the Lord Jesus built his great church on that rock, then perhaps I should build this investigation on a Stone – Stone Harrison."

"*Si Deus vult illud,*" said the Captain showing off his Latin.

"Yes, only if God wills it," parroted the Pope in English. Then he added,

MURDER IN THE VATICAN

"When you have finished up with the murder investigation, at least the preliminaries, I want you to turn it over to your second in command and fly to England. You are to put the case before Dr. Harrison and convince him that he must come and help his Pope with this matter."

"Er... Sir. Stone is not a Catholic."

"What is he then?"

"Raised Church of England, but I doubt he's seen the inside of a church in a very long time. He is ... how should I put it ... an academic first and foremost – a Cambridge don."

"Well, no matter. God loves the wayward ones as well as the saints – maybe more."

****

Captain Celso Palmisano walked up the stairs to Stone Harrison's office in

MURDER IN THE VATICAN

Emmanuel College, Cambridge. It was a large room with bookshelves on every wall, floor to ceiling. The shelves were actually built around the windows to give a view of magnificent gardens below, as well as a pond filled with fish.

Stone said he liked to look at his books and then to gaze at the fishpond. He had two passions – reading and fly fishing.

Stone used some of his political capital at Emmanuel to convince the Provost and then the Bursar to stock the pond with trout. Whenever Stone had a mental block or a fuzzy mind he grabbed his five-weight Winston rod and went down to throw a line or two. He always released the fish back into the pond, usually after saying "thank you sweetheart."

MURDER IN THE VATICAN

Emmanuel College was founded by Sir Walter Mildmay in 1584 on the site of a Dominican priory. In his day Sir Walter was a powerful figure, being Chancellor of the Exchequer to Elizabeth I.

A pious puritan, Sir Walter chose to name the college after Jesus Christ. Since there was already a Christ's College and a Jesus College he chose to name his college Emmanuel, being one of the Lord's biblical names meaning "God [is] with us."

The architecture of Emmanuel College ran from ancient to modern, but Stone's office was in an age-old monastic building and Palmisano had to wend his way up a long flight of stairs to reach the office. The building was too old and small to be fitted with an elevator.

MURDER IN THE VATICAN

Arriving almost out of breath at Harrison's office door, Palmisano knocked.

"Come!"

Palmisano opened the rustic door that squeaked in announcement of entry and he greeted his old friend.

They went over all the events of the time they had been apart. Stone Harrison had a small kitchen in his office and served tea and biscuits and they reminisced some more.

Then Stone said, "So, now that we have all the 'what-have-you-been-doings' out of the way, what brings you all the way from Italy my friend?"

Palmisano decided to be straightforward with Harrison, "The Pope wants to see you."

MURDER IN THE VATICAN

Stone was surprised. "Oh, why would he want to see a Cambridge professor?"

"Because you are also a detective of some repute."

"Not ill repute, I hope."

"Stone, you know that even that American rag, *Time Magazine,* named you Man of the Year when you foiled that ISIS plot in London. That was a classy bit of detective work and though *Time* focused on that singular event, I happen to know that that was only one of your many accomplishments that have saved thousands of lives over the years."

"Did the Pope tell you to inflate my ego to get me down to the Vatican?"

"Let's just say that both the Pontiff and I know of your investigative history."

MURDER IN THE VATICAN

"Why would an old man who lives in the past want me to meet with him?"

Palmisano hesitated. He didn't know where to begin. He had gone over several opening statements on the plane, but he couldn't remember them now. Finely he said, "The Vatican is corrupted with evil."

"So you want me to meet with a man who presides over evil? I'm already confused."

"The Pope is a virtuous and honorable servant of the Lord. He wants to clean up the mess there before he goes to meet his Maker."

"How old is he?"

"87."

"He'd better hurry."

"That's partly why he needs your help Stone. He's desperate."

MURDER IN THE VATICAN

"Something must have triggered all this. He's been Pope for a long time and I've been doing what I do for about as long."

"Pope Martin brought in a young priest named Nathan Mendelsohn to investigate the dirty dealings in the Vatican."

"He's the author of *Crimes of the Early Popes*. I have a copy here somewhere."

"Yes, he was the one."

"Was?"

"He was murdered less than a week ago. What is more when I searched his flat all of his papers and computer had gone missing."

"He must have hit an ecclesiastical nerve."

MURDER IN THE VATICAN

"It would seem so and that is why now the Holy Father wants a crack detective to investigate."

"He wants the murder investigated or the widespread corruption?"

"Both. They are linked, of course."

"Of course." Stone Harrison put his hands together with his fingers interlocked as he often did when thinking. He sat like that for several minutes.

Celso Palmisano knew the man well enough to know to let him alone in his "Sherlock Holmes" trance.

He got up and perused the books on the west wall. He knew that the detective was clearing his mind of any preconceptions. Stone liked to begin an investigation with a *tabula rasa* – a blank slate.

MURDER IN THE VATICAN

After a quarter of an hour of looking at books that he had not read and never would, Palmisano heard from behind him, "I have been struggling with my next book for weeks now. It is perhaps a good time to take a break and let the damn thing settle in the background. Books seem to clean themselves up that way, you know."

Palmisano didn't know, but he was very pleased that the famous detective had chosen to meet with the Pontiff.

That night Palmisano was treated to a fine meal and wine at Emmanuel's High Table in what was simply called "The Hall." The humble appellation of this space at Emmanuel belied its grand history.

The Hall occupied the exact position of the church built by the

MURDER IN THE VATICAN

Dominican Friars in 1238. Religious members feel that when dining at Emmanuel they are sitting on hallowed ground. Secular members see it as sanctified by history.

Palmisano was seated on one of the historic oak benches surrounded by portraits of College Masters of the past. A string quartet played softly to those dining that evening. Wine bottles were opened and shared. God was in His heaven, or so it seemed.

Palmisano loved the ceremonies of Cambridge, only, perhaps, to be exceeded by those in Vatican City.

MURDER IN THE VATICAN

CHAPTER SIX

Nothing was like knowing you were the appetizer for a feast of orgy, that you were what whetted the guests and enticed them to devour.
— Fierce Dolan, *Belle du Nuit: A Collection of Five Erotic Stories.*

Near the village of San Mamete on the shores of Lake Lugano, Franco Lombardi Lippi, the Worshipful Master of P2 or *Propaganda Due*, greeted his guests arriving at his lavish lakeside villa.

The guest list included Bishop Paul Sadowski, the Director of the Vatican Bank, Servio Ganza of the Roman Mafia, Danilo Cavallo, the Director of the Ambrosiano Bank and Cardinal Giovani Donati.

Those were the men more or less connected to Lippi and to the Vatican in

MURDER IN THE VATICAN

a variety of ways, but there were also movie stars, including Marcello de Sica and Roberto Melato. The opera tenor Enrico Carlucci had also been invited, but did not show up. The politician Andrea di Stefano did arrive with two bodyguards, who were told to wait by the car.

More important for the men was the surplus of young women who, in various states of undress lounged around the pool as the guests trickled in. There were young boys too.

Pretending to be lesbians two naked whores made love in the classic 69-position on a large exercise mat next to the pool. Actually, they were pretending to pretend. Few in the worldly crowd even cared to watch.

All of the men at the party were members of *Propaganda Due*. Lippi held such parties that most average folks would call orgies four times a year for key members.

There was a great deal of free food and booze and in the back rooms recreational drugs. If attendees wanted anything more than marijuana and cocaine they had to bring their own.

A band played the day's popular songs and some men danced with the girls, while others played a variety of lawn games that had been set up for the guests.

But the game all the men waited for was Bunga Bunga. It was to take place at the end of the night. Each party featured one of the P2 members who had selected to be the target of Bunga Bunga and on this night it was the Director of the Vatican's financial supervisory body, the AIF or *Autorità di*

MURDER IN THE VATICAN

Informazione Finanziaria – Cardinal Giovani Donate. He had come in street clothes for the occasion. For Bunga Bunga he took them off.

Leading up to Bunga Bunga were exotic dancers, a competitive strip tease performed by girls in police garb, nuns' habits and the uniforms of nurses. There was also pole dancing by nude girls.

Just before Bunga Bunga there was a complete sex act on a poolside mat by a buxom blond and a young man who must have spent a great deal of time at the gym.

The men stood around until the young man came all over the face of the girl and threw money to show their appreciation. Those who could had tight erections by the time of the organism.

MURDER IN THE VATICAN

Bunga Bunga began at one in the morning and involved 20 naked young girls and boys in the pool surrounded by equally nude men. After dancing around in the water chanting imaginary African-style songs that centered on the words "Bunga Bunga," the aroused men paired up with the girl or boy of their choice and exited the pool to attendants offering towels and directions to one of the 20 bedrooms that had been prepared with video cameras, sex toys and Viagra, should that be needed.

In the morning after Bunga Bunga Lippi paid the girls and boys and provided the men with a video of their nighttime sexual endeavors. Lippi always kept a copy for himself in case he needed to influence one of the men in the future by way of blackmail. He didn't like that ugly word and privately thought of it as "video influence."

****

In a very non-Bunga Bunga setting, the Pope's sitting room, Captain Celso Palmisano and Stone Harrison met with Pope Martin. The Pontiff explained why he had brought the unfortunate Father Nathan Mendelsohn to the Vatican and what he had hoped to find out as a result of his investigations.

"My hopes ended when I heard of his murder. I feel so guilty about having him investigate things here. His murder has thrown me into somewhat of a depressed state, I'm afraid. I didn't think there was any hope of continuing the search for evidence of corruption until Captain Palmisano told me about you."

MURDER IN THE VATICAN

Stone Harrison said, "I only hope I can be of service Your Holiness." Palmisano had briefed Stone on the proper way to address the Pope.

"I want you to do two things for the church. First, I would like you to find the killer or killers of Father Mendelsohn. He was a good man and a great scholar. His murder should not go unpunished."

Stone said, "I will do my best."

"Secondly, I want you to continue with the investigations the good Father had begun. It has become clear to me that there are financial irregularities in the Vatican that I lack the expertise to understand or prevent."

"Again, I will do everything in my power to bring these to the light of day Your Holiness."

MURDER IN THE VATICAN

"Good. Our captain speaks highly of you and I appreciate that you have taken leave from the university to come to Italy. I have never been there, but I hear that Cambridge is a beautiful medieval village."

"With some modern conveniences and way too many cars, but yes, I love Cambridge."

"You will stay in the same flat that we gave to Father Mendelsohn, if that is convenient. You are to have complete access to anything and anyone in Vatican City. I have had an envelope with an advance in cash placed on the dining room table in the apartment. Tell me if you need more for expenses. If you run into any blockages or barriers to your investigation, come back and see me. You can do this at any time. Just notify my secretary and he will arrange it."

Captain Palmisano added, "You will also have the complete backing of the *Gendarmeria* here in the Vatican. You already have my office and mobile phone numbers. Call me anytime."

The Pope stood and ended the meeting by saying, "I have arranged for my secretary, Monsignor Corvi, to take you on a tour of Vatican City so that you will know the place and then he will show you to your quarters. Your bags, I believe, have already been delivered to your flat."

Palmisano kissed the Pontiff's ring and Stone shook his hand.

Monsignor Alfio Corvi then helped the Pope back to his quarters. As Stone and the Captain of the *Gendarmeria* waited for him to return the detective

MURDER IN THE VATICAN

said, "The Pope is very frail, but I can see that you were right. He is very sharp mentally. I hope I can help him. He seems determined to ferret out the Vatican's criminals."

"Yes, he wants this done before his term is over."

"I'm going to get to work on it first thing in the morning."

"I've prepared an annotated list of the players I think may be involved. I had my sergeant deliver it to your apartment. It will be on your desk. Go over it and if you have any questions, don't hesitate to call me." Stone Harrison said that he would.

Corvi arrived and spent three hours showing Stone around the Vatican. When the detective was finally escorted to his flat he thanked the secretary for his time and effort and then closed the door to his new digs.

Inside he pocketed the euros the Pope had left and read through the list Palmisano had placed there for him. When he was done he sat and thought about what he had just read. In his mind he was thinking, *This place is a like a medieval dungeon. And Celso is saying there are things going on that are truly criminal. What have I got myself into here?*

If Stone Harrison had received an answer to that question there and then, he may have grabbed his unpacked bags and headed for the airport; instead he set about making himself at home in his little part of the ecclesiastical fortress.

MURDER IN THE VATICAN

CHAPTER SEVEN

Generally speaking, the more money that's involved in anything, the more people are expecting and hoping that it's not going to fail.
– Chris Pine, Actor

The detective Stone Harrison spent two months poking around Vatican City, talking with folks, but mainly doing research in the Vatican Library. He covered much of the same ground as Father Mendelsohn had done.

However, at the beginning of the third month he stumbled on something of a hot potato. He called his friend Celso Palmisano and they met for coffee at the *AntiCafé Roma* near the Vatican. Their thinking was that outside of Vatican City there was less chance of being overheard by members of the Curia.

MURDER IN THE VATICAN

After their coffee came, Palmisano asked, "So I haven't seen you since we met with the Pope. What's up?"

"I think I've stumbled on something significant."

"On the murder?"

"No, something to do with the flow of money through the banks."

"What banks are you talking about?"

"Obviously the Vatican Bank, but also the Ambrosiano Bank. The Vatican is the largest stockholder in that outside bank."

"I didn't know that. Where is its main office?"

"Milan."

Palmisano tried his coffee, but it was way too hot to drink. He put the cup back down, "So what did you find?"

MURDER IN THE VATICAN

"There is a man named Danilo Cavallo who heads it up. He meets regularly with Bishop Sadowski"

Palmisano offered, "He's head of the Vatican Bank, Paul Sadowski. He came from Poland. Quite a financial wizard they say."

"One of the interesting things is that Sadowski and Cavallo have been seeing each other at P2 meetings."

"*Propaganda Due?*"

"Yes."

"But that's forbidden, at least for the Bishop. No member of the Vatican is allowed to belong to a secret society and P2 is a Masonic Lodge and not a very reputable one. Its Worshipful Master is Franco Lombardi Lippi. He's a slippery character, Stone. I know that he is deeply involved in some very dicey politics."

MURDER IN THE VATICAN

"Anyway, word has it that they have been huddling together much more frequently than usual and that is because Ambrosiano Bank is in deep financial trouble."

"Perhaps Cavallo wants Sadowski to bail him out?"

"The question is why is the bank on the skids. It is an old and well-established bank. I looked it up. It was founded in 1896. It has been sound for many decades with ample resources and reserves. It shouldn't be on the rocks."

Palmisano added, "Let me tell you a little gossip I picked up recently that may be pertinent."

"Shoot."

Palmisano tried his coffee again and took a sip. "I heard a rumor that the Vatican Bank is being investigated by the FBI for funneling funds to ISIS. Perhaps re-funneling is a better term."

"The so-called Islamic State? Why would a Christian bank supply a Muslim group of terrorists who want to take over the world? If they did they certainly wouldn't allow the Catholic Church to continue operating. To those radicals Christians are infidels."

"I don't have an answer for that Stone and I don't even know if there is anything to the rumor."

"It couldn't be for ideological reasons, so it has to be for money. Somebody's making a side profit in the deal. I've got to look into that a little deeper."

"Stone, I know that I don't have to mention this, but be careful. Father Mendelsohn was covering some of the

MURDER IN THE VATICAN

same ground as you and look what happened to him."

Stone Harrison patted his heart, "I'm never without Walt."

Celso Palmisano knew that Stone called his Walther Arms PK380 firearm by the nickname "Walt."

"And watch your food. More than one Pope in history has been poisoned."

"I make it a habit not to eat in the Vatican cafeteria."

"Good plan. The food is so bad anyway that you might die from it even without the added poison."

****

The two FBI investigators, Marty Franks and Jack Dennison checked into the *Hotel Amalia Vaticano*, a three-star affair at 66 Via Germanico.

There contact at the Vatican, Captain Celso Palmisano of the Vatican's

MURDER IN THE VATICAN

Gendarmeria was waiting for them in the hotel's café.

As soon as the pair checked in and dropped their bags in their adjoining rooms, they met the police captain, ordering coffee.

"Still a little jet lag," explained Marty Franks.

"Other than that I trust your flight was uneventful."

"Well, not entirely," said Jack Dennison. "There was woman with a crying baby who didn't seem to know how to calm him down."

"That's never pleasant," commiserated Celso.

MURDER IN THE VATICAN

After a few more pleasantries Agent Dennison briefed Captain Palmisano on the reason for their visit to the Vatican.

"Mind you, they're just rumors we've picked up from the European chatter, but we think that perhaps, in some weird way, the Vatican Bank is working with ISIS."

"That would be pretty far fetched, I would have thought," disagreed Palmisano.

"That's what we thought," said Franks, "but we have multiple examples of known ISIS baddies bragging how they have compromised the infidels at the Vatican by using their bank to launder terrorist money."

"That is, of course, hearsay," said Palmisano in a cautionary manner.

MURDER IN THE VATICAN

"We would like you to watch out for any indications that these rumors might be true. We don't have any jurisdiction in the Vatican State or in Italy, so this is just a friendly visit to a colleague. I hope we can work together on this. We'd really like to find any ISIS money trail."

"Follow the money," said Jack Dennison lightly.

Just then Stone Harrison walked into the coffee shop. Celso Palmisano stood and shook his hand, "Thanks for coming Stone."

Palmisano introduced the detective to the two FBI agents and explained that he had invited the Private Investigator to join them because he was working on possible financial malfeasance at the bank."

MURDER IN THE VATICAN

When he was seated and had ordered a beer, Stone asked, "Why is the FBI interested in the Vatican Bank? I thought your Homeland Security folks would handle ISIS matters."

Franks explained that since 9/11 the two agencies had been working together more closely and their boss, FBI Director Eugene Donald, was the President's liaison to Homeland Security. "It's just an exploratory visit. We want to find any threads that could help us cut off terrorist funding. And we want to explore the Mafia angle. That's our primary mandate. We both happen to speak Italian, so we got the gig."

Stone explained that he had also picked up inklings of money laundering at the Vatican Bank and perhaps also through Ambrosiano Bank, but that he had no hard evidence at that point of his investigation. "Mostly I am hearing tidbits at the Mafia, not terrorists."

The law officers and Stone continued to mull over the possibilities and Captain Palmisano promised to wrangle a meeting for the FBI with Bishop Paul Sadowski, of the Vatican Bank.

"We also know that somehow Ambrosiano Bank is involved, so after Rome we're heading up to Milan to see if we can meet with the bank's director."

"That would be Danilo Cavallo," said Celso Palmisano matter-of-factly.

"A slippery eel that one," said Harrison.

"To go along with the snakes at the Vatican," put in Palmisano.

"Snakes and eels. What have we got ourselves into?" asked Marty Franks rhetorically.

MURDER IN THE VATICAN

Cynically, Stone Harrison said, "Some say that international banking is a snake pit."

"And I've heard the same thing about the Vatican," muttered Agent Dennison.

"You don't sound like you're Catholic," commented Celso Palmisano.

Franks added, "Actually, we both are. That's another reason why the director sent us over here."

Jack Dennison clarified, "But we're law enforcement officers, first and foremost."

To himself, Stone Harrison thought, *I'm not sure either a badge or a certificate of baptism is going to help these Yanks.*

****

MURDER IN THE VATICAN

"We have a lot of our money in there," said *Don* Servio Ganza, "that's why I'm both worried and angry."

The head of the Roman Mafia was sitting at the head of a table with the other prominent figures in the crime syndicate. He was explaining the bad news he had just received from Bishop Paul Sadowski, head of the Vatican Bank.

"I'm worried because we could lose millions of Euros. I'm also angry because apparently it's because of the head of Ambrosiano Bank. He's been skimming for himself and has brought his bank to the edge of bankruptcy."

The second in command, Vincenzo Marconi asked, "Wait a minute Servio. What's Ambrosiano Bank got to do with the Vatican Bank? That's where we keep our funds, not Ambrosiano."

MURDER IN THE VATICAN

"It's partly my fault and that's another reason I'm pissed off. Four years ago Sadowski came to me and asked if he could use some of our deposits to help his friend at Ambrosiano Bank. Cavallo had hit a rocky patch over there and Sadowski wanted to help him out. I decided to help Sadowski out and that's how we got to this point."

"So if Ambrosiano Bank goes belly up we lose a bundle? What can we do?"

"Don't go throwing good money after bad," said another man at the table, his Avanti cigar flapping up and down as he talked. No one could ever figure out how Lucio Rotolo could keep the cigar from falling out of his mouth. If he clenched it in his teeth he couldn't talk, but holding it in his lips, as it seemed he did when he talked, was a feat no one else at the table had been able to duplicate – hence his nickname "Lips."

Lucio Rotolo was known as the Mafia's "Cashier" because he was so heavily involved in the financial affairs of the Roman mob. Those seated around the table knew him as "Lips the Cashier." They also knew that he had one of those memories for numbers. If you asked him to add 1,234,345,678 with 543,333,768,964 in a snap he would come up with 544,568,114,642 and if you immediately told him to multiply the two numbers he would come up with some gigantic number and tell you that it was to the 20th power.

The Boss assured the group that he was not contemplating providing either the Vatican Bank or Ambrosiano Bank with any more of the Mafia's money. "Anyway Lips, I would have to come to you, hat in hand, to ask for such funds."

There was nervous laughter around the table because it was a known secret that there was bad blood between the *Don* and Lips the Cashier. No one at the table could ever figure out which one was personally pocketing more of the Mafia's money stream. Each thief thought the other was stealing Mafia funds and both were right.

Vincenzo Marconi tried to bring the discussion back to the problem at hand, "Again, what're we gonna to do about it if we're not gonna to bail the bastards out?"

A mobster at the other end of the table suggested, "A little visit?"

Another chimed in, "Some persuasion?"

MURDER IN THE VATICAN

It was Mafia meta-talk for some strong-arm stuff.

****

After a fine seafood dinner Danilo Cavallo was just coming out of the classy *Ristorante Piazza Repubblica* and was waiting on the *Via Aldo Manuzio* for his Mercedes to be brought around when a black van pulled up in front of Cavallo who had that night's whore on his arm.

A sliding door opened and two Mafioso popped out. One hit Cavallo on the head with a lead sap and he went directly to la-la land. The other one punched the girl in the face, a blow that caused several thousand Euros worth of reconstructive surgery bills. She collapsed in a heap and the two gorillas gripped the limp body of the head of Ambrosiano Bank and unceremoniously tossed it into the back of the van, which immediately sped off almost before the thugs could get the door slid shut.

Seven hours later Danilo Cavallo was thrown from the same van, which kindly slowed down to 20 miles per hour for the toss. He landed in a stack of garbage. That he had been deposited at the Milan Municipal Dump was part of the message. The other part of the message was all over his face written in blood, welts and cuts.

His evening in captivity had been interspersed with blows from men expert at delivering messages that didn't require proper grammar or big words. All in all, the message was, "Get your fucking act together and give us our money back – or else!"

MURDER IN THE VATICAN

CHAPTER EIGHT

Joking cements a relationship
–   Anthropological Axiom

Cardinal Giovani Donati had donned civilian clothes to meet with Franco Lippi at the *Propaganda Due* lodge. When he arrived Bishop Paul Sadowski was there and was also in plain clothes.

Lippi began, "So tell us what happened."

He was addressing Donati who replied, "It seems our mobster friends paid *Signore* Cavallo a visit."

"Of the Mafia kind, I suppose," said Sadowski.

"They roughed him up pretty good. Mostly just scared him. They want their money back."

MURDER IN THE VATICAN

"Are we next?" asked Bishop Paul Sadowski, a little shaken by the news.

"I don't think those thugs would stoop to harming a member of the Curia," said Donati trying to paint a rosy color on the situation.

"I wouldn't be too sure," warned Lippi. "When it comes to money the Mafioso seem to forget the *Marquess of Queensberry rules*, if they even knew the rules that have governed gentlemanly forms of fisticuffs since 1867."

"Yeah, they don't send "Gentleman Jim" Corbett to deliver a message," quipped Donati.

"It's Cavallo that's the problem. He has been sucking Ambrosiano Bank dry for years. If it goes under the Church is going to lose a ton of euros and so would the Roman Mafia."

MURDER IN THE VATICAN

Sadowski fumbled with the pack and lit up a cigarette to try to calm his nerves.

"We're all a little upset by this thing." Lippi went to the small bar and grabbed a bottle of Anisette and three glasses. He set the glasses on the table and poured out three portions of the liqueur. "Drink up gentlemen. It's not all bad. We can fix this thing."

Franco Lombardi Lippi didn't know how wrong he was.

****

Mark Murphy was watching Danilo Cavallo, as he had been instructed by Stone Harrison, when he saw the girl get punched in the face and Cavallo abducted by two heavies.

Murphy was a student Private Investigator that showed a lot of promise in Stone's classes at Cambridge. Harrison had hired him to do some of

MURDER IN THE VATICAN

the outside legwork for him on what he was calling "the Vatican Murder Case."

As he was relating what had happened, Murphy told Stone, "I tried to follow the van, but by the time I reached my Fiat and got it started, they were gone. So I went over and helped the girl. She was bleeding from the nose pretty profusely."

MURDER IN THE VATICAN

"Did you get a good look at the men? Could you recognize them again?"

"Possibly, but it was dark and they were moving all the time. They had duct tape over the license plate. One of them had a nose like a hawk. I remember that.   They roughed Cavallo up pretty badly though."

"Right there on the street?"

"No, they just threw him in and sped off."

"So how do you know that they beat him?"

"After I got the girl to the hospital I went to his house and waited."

"And?"

"And several hours later a taxi pulled up and Cavallo limped out. His face looked like a lump of hamburger. One arm was not working all that well when he tried to pay the cabbie."

MURDER IN THE VATICAN

"Good work Mark. Something's going on here, but I don't know what."

Murphy asked, "This guy is a big shot at the Ambrosiano Bank?"

"The top guy. The Director."

"I read the file on the Vatican Bank. They're invested pretty heavily in Cavallo's bank."

"I don't know, but it's a bit of a stretch to think that Sadowski or Donati would hire thugs to beat up Cavallo. And if they did, why? And remember, somebody murdered Father Mendelsohn."

"Maybe it's unrelated to the Vatican Bank. Maybe Cavallo just pissed somebody off. It could have been unconnected to banking or to the Vatican."

"I think not," said Stone as he played with his meerschaum pipe. He

MURDER IN THE VATICAN

had given up smoking his pipe years ago, but always carried it with him, sort of like prayer beads in the Middle East. He could finger the pipe and concentrate better, for some strange reason. "I think Sadowski, Donati and Cavallo are all interconnected in some way and we know that there are rumors that the Vatican Bank is laundering Mafia money. The FBI thinks so anyway. It could have been Mafioso that grabbed him."

"That makes sense," reasoned Murphy, "if the Mafia has money in the Vatican Bank and the Vatican Bank is invested in the Ambrosiano Bank and Cavallo's bank is in financial trouble, then the Mafioso could be at risk as well as Sadowski."

"Makes sense. Look Murf, I want you to stick tight on Cavallo. I want to know who he goes to see once he licks his wounds."

"Murf the Smurf is on it boss."

"I don't like it when you call me boss."

"I don't like it when you call me Murf."

"It's a standoff, I guess."

"I guess so ... boss."

"You know after you go I'm going to say 'Murf."

"But I won't hear it so it doesn't count."

If a social anthropologist had been listening to the two detectives he would have concluded that they had a joking relationship. He would have known that A. R. Radcliffe-Brown, an early 20th century anthropologist, had written about such ritualized banter between certain categories of individuals in primitive societies, as they were called then.

Furthermore, he would have known that anthropologists call the kind of joking between Stone and Mark "symmetrical joking," the kind in which each makes fun at the expense of the other and both enjoy the banter because it is a sign of strong positive affect in their relationship.

The joking relationship is an interaction that mediates and stabilizes relationships where there is the possibility of conflict or tension. The joking lessens the chance of that competition breaking out in the open.

Both Stone and Murphy would experience lots of conflict, but of a larger and more dangerous kind than a simple tiff between friends.

MURDER IN THE VATICAN

CHAPTER NINE

*Man is not, by nature, deserving of all that he wants.
When we think that we are automatically entitled to
something; that is when we start walking all over
others to get it.*
– Chris Jami,
Diotima, Battery, Electric Personality

Ercole Donati was the First Mate on the Dutch slaving ship, the *Wildvuur,* returning to Amsterdam from the Americas where they exchanged their slaves for a load of tobacco and sugar. It was 1740 and the ship's Captain who had been ill died on the way back to Europe. Consequently Ercole Donati, an ancestor to Cardinal Giovani Donati, stole the valuable cargo by diverting the ship to Naples.

Ercole Donati then invested the money from the sale of the tobacco and sugar in a small army of brigands who began to terrorize farmers in the province of Viterbo outside of Rome. By killing many and driving out others, Ercole Donati managed to carve out a large estate for himself and his descendants, one of which rose to become a Cardinal in the Holy Roman Church – Giovani Donati.

Unfortunately for that Cardinal, who had become the sole remaining member of the Donati line, his vast estate became the subject of an investigation by a law student at the *Università degli Studi della Tuscia* in Viterbo as part of his master's thesis.

The student, Colombo Fiscella graduated with honors and, being independently wealthy, chose to pursue the case of the Donati estate for the benefit of the families that had been displaced in the 18th century rampage by Ercole Donati.

The young *Avvocato* strove to become the *rappresentante legale* for the living members of those farm families that had their land stolen from them.

Cardinal Giovani Donati became aware of the threat to his estate when the attorney filed his first lawsuit at the Palace of Justice in Rome. He immediately met with his lawyer to determine if the young man had a good case against him. He did.

The Cardinal tried to get his attorney to go up against Colombo Fiscella, but his *Avvocato* said it was useless, "You will most likely lose your land. In this modern age there is a sentiment against wealthy landowners and your estate is the largest in central Italy."

"It's the goddamned communists on the bench. That's what Italy has come to, a damnable communist state no better than Russia."

"Nevertheless, they can take your land."

"It's been in the family since 1745, for Christ's sake!" Donati was overwrought and his blood pressure went to 299 over 77. The blood vessels in his neck were pulsing like the old steam engine locomotives.

Authoritatively, the attorney said, "There is nothing that can legally be done to stop these lawsuits. In my judgment, this is just the first of many. When family number one gets their land back, Colombo Fiscella will move on to family number two's case and so on till your entire estate has been dismantled."

It was the attorney's words "nothing that can legally be done" that stuck in the Cardinal's mind.

****

Colombo Fiscella was having dinner at the street café called *La Fraschetta Nel Parco*, dining alone because his girlfriend, Tara Bracco, was meeting with a client. She was also an attorney.

Fiscella was eating his *Penne Pasta in Arrabbiata Sauce* when a motorcyclist pulled alongside his table and fired three fatal shots into him. The cyclist sped off and was never caught.

When she had recovered from the shock and grief over Colombo Fiscella's murder, Tara Bracco vowed to take up the case that had been placed before the High Court.

A week after she first appeared in court her body was discovered in a ditch along the *Via Vitellia* near the *Parrocchia di San Pancrazio*, an ancient basilica founded by Pope Symmachus in the 6th century. She had been stabbed to death and her mouth was sewn shut, her lips pierced with 60 pound braided fishing line.

After the two murders of the young attorneys no other Italian lawyer stepped forward to take up the case and the High Court dismissed it.

MURDER IN THE VATICAN

CHAPTER TEN

The intellectual climate of the 1970s, for which the 1950s had already paved the way, contributed to this. A theory was even finally developed at that time that pedophilia should be viewed as something positive. Above all, however, the thesis was advocated–and this even infiltrated Catholic moral theology–that there was no such thing as something that is bad in itself. There were only things that were "relatively" bad. What was good or bad depended on the consequences.

In such a context, where everything is relative and nothing intrinsically evil exists, but only relative good and relative evil, people who have an inclination to such behavior are left without any solid footing. Of course pedophilia is first rather a sickness of individuals, but the fact that it could become so active and so widespread was linked also to an intellectual climate through which the foundations of moral theology, good and evil, became open to question in the Church. Good and evil became interchangeable; they were no longer absolutely clear opposites.

— Pope Benedict XVI, *Light of the World: The Pope, the Church and the Sign of the Times*

Cardinal Giovani Donati had been furious when he realized that Stone

MURDER IN THE VATICAN

Harrison was installed in the apartment of the previous investigator that he had paid to have killed. "That asshole Pope has brought in another peeping tom. An English Private Investigator for Christ's sake."

Bishop Paul Sadowski of the Vatican Bank was not happy either, but a little less hotheaded than the Cardinal. "We dealt with Father Mendelsohn and we can deal with this guy. He is just a Private Investigator and has blood in his veins like Mendelsohn."

MURDER IN THE VATICAN

"My spies tell me that he is in cahoots with Captain Palmisano of our own *Gendarmeria*. Now we've got outsiders and insiders working against us. It's getting a bit costly paying those fucking Mafioso to off all these guys. Ganza wanted five hundred thousand euros for Father Mendelsohn."

"We've got the money Giovani. Relax."

"You know I never relax. We've woven a fine web here and we damn well better be sure we don't get caught in it."

"Maybe the PI is just looking into Mendelsohn's murder – nothing more."

"I've got my guys watching him. If he turns out to be more than that we've got to go back to Ganza and I hate that part. Skimming money is one thing, but killing scares me. It's a mortal sin."

MURDER IN THE VATICAN

Paul Sadowski had known the Cardinal a long time and knew that he meant that he was in fear of his eternal soul. Part of Donati was the lusty man who liked to fuck young boys and live the highlife; but there was still a part of him that feared God and believed that his Heavenly Father could see all of his sins. Some were forgivable, like pocketing church funds, but murder ... that might lead to the fire and brimstone.

Once Donati had told Sadowski about a recurring dream he had. In it he was on a beach sunbathing, as the Cardinal liked to do in the Canary Islands, but although he enjoyed the heat of the sun, the heat in the dream was like that of a thousand suns and what was worse was that the burning sensation on his skin was accompanied by the smell of sulfur.

A reader of the Bible, Cardinal Donati knew that the ancient word for sulfur was brimstone.

****

Adalberto Bartalotti was intent on providing Cardinal Donati a little sulfur smell in this life. Bartalotti worked for Franco Lombardi Lippi, the Worshipful Master of *Propaganda Due.* He had taken a certificate in video technology from the *Politecnico di Roma* and Lippi hired him on a contract basis to set up, repair and operate his secret video recorders in the rooms he provided his Bunga Bunga guests.

In one room of Lippi's mansion there was a setup to process the DVDs Lippi provided for his guests after their night of pleasure.

MURDER IN THE VATICAN

Four times a year Bartalotti was brought in a day in advance of the parties to make sure that all the equipment was in good working order. Then, during the night, when the men were with their whores, he had to be sure that the machines kept running and change out the DVDs as required.

He had done this for two years before he asked Lippi to double his fee. When Lippi refused, Bartalotti decided to go into business for himself. He started with Cardinal Giovani Donati.

Bartalotti sent Donati a copy of a video showing him fucking a young boy of eight whose hands were handcuffed to the bedposts and who was spread-eagled on his stomach with his feet roped to the bedposts at the foot of the bed. A pillow had been placed under the boy's hips to raise his ass into a position where it was easy for the portly Donati to insert his penis into the boy's asshole.

Watching the DVD Bartalotti was surprised that the old Cardinal was able to come twice that night – once in the boy's anus and once in his mouth.

The newly minted entrepreneur sent the DVD to the Cardinal at the Vatican by special currier along with a letter demanding fifty thousand euros not to provide Rome's *Rete Oro* TV channel with a copy of the DVD.

****

Cardinal Giovani Donati stormed into the chambers of the Worshipful Master of P2 shouting, "What the fuck is going on Franco?"

Franco Lippi was startled, "What do you mean?"

The Cardinal shoved the letter in front of his face, "This. Read it."

MURDER IN THE VATICAN

Lippi took the letter and read it, "This wasn't me Franco, but I think I know who it is."

"Who for God's sake?"

"My video technician. He's the only one with access to the videos."

"I thought the videos were just for the guests."

"DVD's can be copied. He must have made a copy of yours." Lippi didn't tell the Cardinal that he also kept copies in a special vault for use not unlike his video technician had laid on the Prelate.

"The bastard wants fifty thousand euros!" Donati's face was beet red and the veins in his temples stood out like a freighter's anchor ropes.

"Stay calm Giovani. How does he propose that you pay him?"

"It's there in the letter."

"I only read the first part."

MURDER IN THE VATICAN

"He wants me to deliver it to that postal box he mentions in the letter."

"Then he will have to retrieve it, won't he?"

The Cardinal dropped his shoulders, which had been up around his ears with tension, "I guess. Yeah, we can get him then."

"Leave it up to me. I created this problem for you, so let me solve it. You deliver a package stuffed with newspaper or some such thing and when he goes to get it I'll have a man watching."

The Worshipful Master thought that the Cardinal was going to cry. He hugged Lippi and thanked him profusely. "This would have ruined me Franco. Thank you."

****

MURDER IN THE VATICAN

When Adalberto Bartalotti picked up his package at the *Ufficio Postale* he didn't open it. He merely tucked it under his arm, smiled and strode out into the evening.

It was a warm autumn night in Rome and he could see the Coliseum all lit up for the tourists. He couldn't wait to get back to his tiny Fiat Panda to count it or at least just look at the bills.

The goon following Bartalotti knew that he would never make it to the car.

MURDER IN THE VATICAN

CHAPTER ELEVEN

*It is easier to rob by setting up a bank than
by holding up a bank clerk.*
– Bertolt Brecht, German Playwright & Poet

Caliph Abu Bakr al Baghdadi,
leader of ISIS, the Islamic State of Iraq
and al-Sham, sat on a rug in his tent in
an undisclosed location in Syria. Across
from him on a smaller rug was Abu
Salah, his Finance Minister.

The self-proclaimed Caliph was
speaking, "What is the latest cash
count?"

Abu Salah replied, "It is more or
less eight million US dollars, also some is
in euros along with various other
currencies. As you know, we always try
to get as much hard currency as
possible. Most is in dollars and euros."

MURDER IN THE VATICAN

"I want to purchase some shoulder-fired missiles. One hundred RPG-7s, to be exact. The Bulgarian sellers want hard currency sent electronically to their bank and not cash, so we have to launder the money. They prefer dollars, but will take euros too. Here is the account number of the Bulgarian bank. We can't send cash. We need to send it by wire transfer as soon as possible." Caliph Baghdadi handed over a notepad with the number written on it.

"I will contact our man at the Vatican Bank. We will have to ship the cash to Bishop Sadowski as we always do, labeled as religious books."

"How will you route it?"

"We change it each time. This time I think I'll send it to Bagdad and our man at Bagram Air Base will send it on to London. From there it goes to Rome or more specifically to the Vatican City in Rome."

"And you change the labeling all along the route."

"Of course. We don't want a large shipment of books coming into the Vatican postmarked from Syria. We own that bookstore in London and that's the address anyone snooping would see."

"How long will it take to make the deposit in the United Bulgarian Bank?"

"At this point," replied Abu Salah, "I cannot say for sure. I have to notify our man in London. He has to fly down to Rome and talk with Sadowski. This is a big deposit and we have to be sure the Christians are on the same page as we are."

MURDER IN THE VATICAN

"But we are reading the *Qur'ān* and they are reading the Bible," joked the Caliph, a rare bit of levity from the otherwise dour man.

Abu Salah fired back, "When it comes to money there is only one text."

"I suppose that is Adam Smith's *The Wealth of Nations*." Caliph Abu Bakr al Baghdadi had read this as part of his Ph.D taken in Bagdad before he became radicalized and founded ISIS.

"It's as close to a sacred text for capitalists as any, I guess." Abu Salah had read it too while completing his Masters Degree in finance at Oxford University.

Back to business, Caliph Abu Bakr al Baghdadi said, "Let me know when the transfer is complete."

MURDER IN THE VATICAN

"I'll get on it right away and it should go smoothly and hopefully quickly, *Insha'Allah* – If Allah wills."

****

Anthony Aylmer got the message from the ISIS group in Syria. He was instructed to close up the bookstore and fly to Rome to meet with Bishop Paul Sadowski – Head of the Vatican Bank.

He was to ask if they would be willing to launder $8,139, 421 for ISIS. He loved these deals because he took a three percent cut and he knew that Sadowski must do the same, though he didn't know the percentage the Bishop took for himself.

On the plane the bookish Aylmer took out his calculator and computed his fee. It came to $244,182.63. *Being a nice guy*, he thought, *I'll drop the 63 cents.* He chuckled so loud that two

nearby passengers looked askance at
him and one contemplated moving to
another seat.

****

When Anthony Aylmer met with
Bishop Sadowski the Bank Director
agreed to take the money. He felt it was
good for relations with ISIS, in case they
actually took over the world – which he
saw as unlikely; and more importantly
he was able to calculate in his head his
personal five percent cut – $406,971.05.
He too would drop the nickel.

Nevertheless, Sadowski expressed
some trepidation, "We have to be very
circumspect on this Mr. Aylmer. If word
ever got out that the Vatican Bank was
doing business with Islamic terrorists –
well, you can imagine the uproar it
would create internationally. At best
the Pope would fire me and it is not out

MURDER IN THE VATICAN

of the realm of possibility that he would have me killed."

Anthony Aylmer wasn't sure that modern Popes went around doing such Machiavellian things as murder anymore, although he had read enough history to know that it was a practice in ancient times. Nonetheless, he nodded in agreement.

Sadowski went on, "I would like you to send the cash in five different shipments so as not to raise any eyebrows with a large one coming in."

"I can do that," agreed the bookstore owner. "We do a shipment of our books every Wednesday and I will include yours in the orders over the next five weeks, or maybe six if ISIS doesn't get me the cash on time."

****

MURDER IN THE VATICAN

Interpol Head Agent Ernest Bradbury-Holmes was drinking beer in Bradbury-Holmes's favorite pub, *The Harwood Arms* on London's Walham Grove Street. With him was his junior partner, George Wolitzer, a Senior Agent.

Based in Lyon, France Interpol was the International Criminal Police Organization that operated to combat crime in Europe. These two agents worked out of the London office.

Bradbury-Holmes was saying, "We've been following this bugger for months and it finally paid off. Good job George."

George Wolitzer had had a tail on the owner of *Page One Books* and his men finally followed him to the Vatican Bank. A tap on his phone had also revealed his links to someone in Syria. They assumed it was an ISIS contact.

"We don't have definitive evidence of a link between the Vatican and ISIS, but we have lots of smoke."

"Is Anthony Aylmer still in Rome?"

"No. He's on a plane back to London as we speak."

"Any idea what he is doing down there?"

"Not definitive, but my suspicion is aroused by the fact that he regularly communicates with Syria in ways that can only be coded messages and now he visits with the director at the Vatican Bank, a financial institution thought to be involved in money laundering."

"It would seem that two and two add up to four."

"That's my math Ernest."

MURDER IN THE VATICAN

The Head Agent went to the bar and ordered two more pints of bitters. When he came back he pushed one pint over to his colleague and said, "If they are laundering ISIS cash he should be getting something from Syria soon."

"When he does he will re-box it and send it on to Rome. We can nail him with the cash or let him send it on to the Vatican Bank."

"Here in London is a lot easier."

George Wolitzer said, "I have men watching the bookstore and I am alerting the head of the Vatican *Gendarmerie* about the possible shipment of cash to the Vatican Bank."

Bradbury-Holmes asked, "What's his name?"

"Captain Celso Palmisano."

"Good man?"

MURDER IN THE VATICAN

"Cambridge trained in law enforcement. Not your average palace guard, I would have thought."

"Right. Keep me informed George."

"Right sir."

"No 'Sirs' over beer George. Drink up."

"Right."

MURDER IN THE VATICAN

CHAPTER TWELVE

Crime is terribly revealing. Try and vary your methods as you will, your tastes, your habits, your attitude of mind, and your soul is revealed by your actions.
– Agatha Christie

Captain Celso Palmisano met for coffee with Stone Harrison in the *Antico Caffè San Pietro* near the Vatican.

"What's up?" asked Stone. "On the phone it sounded like this was something important."

"It may or may not be Stone. I got a message from an Interpol colleague. He says that they are monitoring an owner of a bookstore in London who they suspect has links with ISIS."

"Interesting, but what does that have to do with the Vatican?"

MURDER IN THE VATICAN

"It seems that this bloke flew down here and met with Sadowski."

"A bookstore owner flew down to the Vatican Bank? That seems a little off base."

"Doesn't it. They think he is a messenger of some sort – an ISIS messenger."

"Is he a Muslim or of Middle Eastern descent?'

"No, I don't think so. His name is Anthony Aylmer."

"Hmmm." Stone Harrison was fiddling with his meerschaum pipe and thinking. Palmisano took the time to light up a filtered *Nazionali* cigarette. It was an unusually warm November evening and they were sitting on the street patio.

After blowing smoke into the night air Palmisano said, "I respect your

MURDER IN THE VATICAN

courage in stopping smoking. I can't seem to bring it off. I guess I need a meerschaum pipe or something like that."

"The pipe doesn't keep me from smoking. It is just a device I use to focus my thoughts."

Palmisano took another deep pull on his *Nazionali* and asked, "And what does the pipe tell you about our bookstore mystery man?"

"Not much at this point, but I don't think he traveled all the way down to Italy to talk about books with Bishop Sadowski."

"No, if his ISIS link is valid then talking with the head of the Vatican bank must have something to do with money, don't you think Stone?"

"That *is* what I think. And the kind of money would be cash and probably

136

lots of it. ISIS has billions from oil sales, taxation of the people it has conquered and even from the illegal sale of stolen antiquities and artifacts."

"And they are getting donations from wealthy benefactors in Kuwait, Qatar, and Saudi Arabia, but they can't go and deposit that money in Barclays Bank in London or Wells Fargo in New York."

Stone agreed, "Not a large amount of cash they couldn't. I know that in the United States the red flags go up for the IRS and other government agencies like Homeland Security when a person makes a cash deposit of $10,000 or more in a day, even if they break it up into smaller amounts at different banks."

"What about in the UK?" asked Palmisano.

MURDER IN THE VATICAN

"As far as I know they don't set a specific limiting amount as they do in the USA, but if you show up with a large wad of cash they will ask for accounting documentation to show that you obtained the cash legally."

"That would seem more flexible."

"But not as flexible as the Vatican Bank can be. I have had my suspicions that Sadowski may be laundering money. The Vatican Bank is ideal for it because there are no audits by any outside authority."

"As head of the Vatican's financial supervisory body – the *Autorità di Informazione Finanziaria* – Cardinal Donati is supposed to watch out for just that kind of mischief at the bank."

"There's another character I distrust. That's like putting the fox in charge of the chicken coop Celso."

MURDER IN THE VATICAN

"I would have to agree."

"We've got to put a 24/7 surveillance watch on Sadowski to see if the bookseller makes contact again, or if he starts receiving any shipments from London."

Palmisano said, "I can do that. I'll get my men on it first thing in the morning."

"Do you have people who can tail him without being seen? We don't want to spook him."

"I do. The *Gendarmeria* has a special unit with men trained in surveillance."

"Good," said Harrison. He drained his coffee cup and put his pipe in his pocket. "I think I'll go do some reading and hopefully fall asleep."

Palmisano stood up to and asked, "What are you reading?"

MURDER IN THE VATICAN

"Agatha Christie. Who else? I'm a fan of Hercule Poirot."

"Stone, you're a true gumshoe right up to the moment you fall asleep."

"And beyond. I'll probably dream tonight about radicalized Muslims and bookish Londoners running around Vatican City."

As Palmisano patted Stone on the shoulder he said, "And that's a real nightmare."

Both men left the café laughing, but their musings were not too far off the mark.

MURDER IN THE VATICAN

CHAPTER THIRTEEN

*Religion is so frequently a source of confusion in
political life, and so frequently dangerous to
democracy, precisely because it introduces absolutes
into the realm of relative values.*
— Reinhold Niebuhr, Theologian

The Private Investigator Stone
Harrison woke the next morning
thinking that he needed to know more
about the ideas of ISIS if he was going to
be dealing with them as part of his
investigation. Therefore he caught a taxi
to the large *Mosque of Rome* in the
Roman suburb of Parioli.

There he was introduced to
Imam Muhammad Hassan Ridwan.
They sat in a small room off the Main
Hall where worshipers prayed five times
a day.

MURDER IN THE VATICAN

Once seated Harrison explained that he wanted to understand ISIS eschatology, their beliefs about the end of the world.

Imam Ridwan said that he could do that in general terms, but that he disagreed with the radical terrorism of the ISIS leadership.

"No, I understand," said the Private Investigator. "I just need to know what I'm dealing with in my work."

"Well, fundamentally, they believe that by fomenting more chaos and terror in the world that they can fulfill the prophesies of the ancients."

"What are those prophesies?"

"There are many in both the Qur'ān and the Bible, but they more or less say the same thing. The world is supposed to become very corrupt and move away from the teachings of the Lord – be He Jesus or Allah."

"That's kind of hard to judge, isn't it? The world has never been very pure if you read history."

"ISIS believes that the prophesied redeemer or *Mahdi* has come to earth in the form of Caliph Abu Bakr al Baghdadi."

"He's the ISIS leader, right?"

"Yes, but most Muslims do not accept that he is the *Mahdi*."

"So if the Caliph says the end is nigh, then in their belief system it is."

"Yes, and they believe that they can hurry it along by going to war against all infidels."

Stone said, "Those are non-Muslims, right?"

"No, the ISIS leaders follow a very strict version of Islam, a sect really.

MURDER IN THE VATICAN

They adhere to jihadist principles like *Al-Qaeda* and many other modern-day terrorist groups, but their ideological roots can be traced to Wahhabism."

"Now I'm getting confused with all these terms," said Harrison.

"You don't need to remember them," assured Ridwan. "Just remember that they are ultra-conservatives who believe in the literal interpretation of the scriptures and want a world governed by *Sharia* Law."

"I know about *Sharia*. It's the rule of human life based on religious prophecy rather than manmade legislation."

"Correct.

"So I'm dealing with men who want to launder money which is illegal by man's laws, but they don't recognize those laws."

MURDER IN THE VATICAN

"No they don't. In fact, they believe that anything they can do to create more evil, sin, chaos and corruption in the world the better."

"That doesn't seem to fit with a strong religious belief."

"For ISIS it is a temporary means to a religious end – a world purified by widespread warfare between the forces of good and the forces of evil. It would be their brand of radical Islam against all infidels, which can include Muslims like me and my congregation."

"I guess they define themselves as the good guys."

The cleric laughed. "The White Hats as the Americans say."

"I find it a bit strange that they are using the Vatican Bank to clean their money. It's a Christian institution."

MURDER IN THE VATICAN

"Oh, for ISIS that's no problem. Even their suicide bombers in Europe and America are told that it is perfectly acceptable for them to sin in order to provide them cover from the authorities. You remember 9/11."

"Who doesn't?"

"Well, then you remember Mohamed Atta, the hijacker of American Airlines Flight 11. He and his accomplices went to whore houses, drank alcohol and cavorted in the very ways that the jihadists detest, but the terrorist leaders condoned and paid for that sinful behavior because they felt it was justified in order to deflect any attention by law enforcement. Atta was just supposed to appear as any whore-mongering youth."

"So laundering money through a Christian bank is not sinful."

146

MURDER IN THE VATICAN

"No, it is probably seen as a perfect cover for their activities. Who would believe that terrorist Muslims were sending their cash to the Vatican Bank."

"At the other end, though, the Christian bank director has to be sinning, don't you think?"

"By Biblical or *Qur'ānic* standards, yes; but ISIS would see that as a side benefit."

"What do you mean?"

"Again, the more sinful they can make the world the closer they think they are to the end of the world and the bringing of rule by Allah."

"*Sharia* paradise."

"The fundamentalist Christians call it the *Rapture*. First you get the apocalypse, then God intercedes and all is made well."

MURDER IN THE VATICAN

"Imam, you are a religious scholar. What do you think about all of this?"

"I think that perhaps ISIS is part of the evil that the scriptures predict. Beyond that, I'll just keep praying for a better world. Bullets and bombs are not the answer and most Muslims would agree with me."

"I read that ISIS kills more Muslims than Christians in their reign of terror."

"It is true. As I said, they are part of the problem, not the solution."

Stone Harrison thanked the Imam for his time and insights and caught a cab back to Vatican City. He had a lot to think about.

MURDER IN THE VATICAN

CHAPTER FOURTEEN

Rather fail with honor than succeed by fraud.
– Sophocles

Danilo Cavallo met Cardinal Donati at the *Old Trafford Pub*, just near to the Vatican. He had already consumed three whiskies before the Cardinal, dressed in civilian clothes, walked through the door.

Donati was shocked when he saw the cuts and bruises on Cavallo's face. "What happened to you?"

Cavallo explained about the abduction and beating. "When they were done pounding on me they threw me from a moving vehicle and I landed in the goddamned dump."

Cardinal Donati recognized this as a Mafia message *–rifiuti a spazzatura –* garbage to garbage.

MURDER IN THE VATICAN

Confirming the notion that the Vatican consumes more wine per capita than anywhere in the world the Cardinal ordered a red wine. Cavallo was on his fourth whisky-on-the-rocks.

When his glass of wine came Donati took a sip and then asked, "Do you know who did this?"

"I have a pretty good idea," said Cavallo as he lit up a *Nazionali* cigarette.

"Me too," confirmed Cardinal Donati.

"Why is the Mafia pissed off at me?"

"Danilo, for Christ's sakes, you know we put their money in your bank. You should have kept your fingers out of the till. Now look at the state of Ambrosiano. If the bank goes under they stand to suffer a loss. If that happens you better move to South

MURDER IN THE VATICAN

America and they're going to be coming around to the Vatican looking for a refund. This is not good for any of us. You fucked up."

Cavallo hung his head like a naughty schoolboy. "Can't you shift some funds around and help me out of this?"

"We've done that more than once with the same result. How long can this go on Danilo?"

"Who can I go to if not you? The church has lots of money."

"Yes, the church has lots of money and that money is for things other than supporting your pilfering of Ambrosiano Bank. What the hell are you doing with all that money? How many whores can you fuck? Are you on drugs? What is going on with you?"

MURDER IN THE VATICAN

Danilo Cavallo was staring at the remaining ice in his empty whiskey glass. He stayed that way for several minutes and Donati let him stew. Finally, he asked, "Who else can I go to?"

Donati expected this question and had a ready answer, "Try Franco."

"Lippi?"

"P2 has a treasure chest. Try them. You're a member. Maybe Lippi will help you out of this predicament. I've got to go. I've got an appointment." He stood up and drained his glass.

Donati was lying and Cavallo knew he was lying. He knew that his handouts from the Vatican Bank had just been cut off. As the Cardinal walked through the door Cavallo was whimpering and raised his hand to the barkeep signaling that he wanted another whiskey.

MURDER IN THE VATICAN

Bishop Paul Sadowski and P2's Franco Lippi lounged by the elaborate swimming pool at *Sandals Royal Bahamian Spa Resort & Offshore Island* in the Caribbean. They were on a two-week vacation; one of four they took each year.

Each man had a pretty light-skinned mulato girl next to him and a small band played as they danced and swam in the luxurious resort. All the band members were in Bermuda shorts and brightly colored shirts with birds and animals on them. The images almost seemed alive as the musicians pounded out their music.

When the song was over the Bishop said, "Hey Franco. I'm going up to my room for a while. Time for a little Bunga Bunga."

MURDER IN THE VATICAN

The slim girl on his arm looked at him and asked, "What is Bunga Bunga."

"Sweetie," said the Vatican Curate, "I'm about to show you. Every day I'm going to show you. By the time I leave this island you're going to be Bunga Bunga-ed out."

****

Danilo Cavallo had a flat in London and when he sobered up he caught a flight to Heathrow and then a taxi to 3098 Chalk Farm Road in Camden Town.

Cavallo had decided to make a run for it. He fled Rome using a false passport with the name of Gian Roberto Calvini. He shaved off his prominent mustache and bleached his hair blond.

He couldn't find Lippi and had nowhere else to go to find funds to save Ambrosiano Bank. His only hope was to regroup and take the money he had squirreled away in London and find a quiet place in Africa or South America to start over.

****

Two days later a postal clerk was crossing Blackfriars Bridge near the financial district of London. He was idly staring at a piece of snarled driftwood floating in the dirty water of the Thames River and noticed a body of a man hanging from the scaffolding beneath the bridge.

When the police lowered the body of Danilo Cavallo they found that his clothing was stuffed with bricks and he was carrying around $56,000 in three different currencies. He also had a one-way first class ticket to the Seychelles Islands in the Indian Ocean off the coast of East Africa.

MURDER IN THE VATICAN

The weight of the bricks had broken Cavallo's neck and severed his spinal column. His skin had stretched so much that in death the five foot nine banker became well over six foot tall.

MURDER IN THE VATICAN

CHAPTER FIFTEEN

*The Vatican is like a huge kind of magician's club.
The more you look into it the more awful it becomes.
And they're laughing at us. That's when I get angry.*
– Peter Mullan, Scottish Actor

Stone Harrison read about the strange death of the Ambrosiano Bank Director, Danilo Cavallo, while reading the *London Times* in the *Bibliotheca Apostolica Vaticana* – the Vatican Library.

He stepped out into the *Cortile della Biblioteca*, found a bench and made a call on his mobile phone. While he waited for Captain Palmisano to answer his phone he watched the pigeons picking at the crumbs of the bread someone had thrown on the courtyard grass. There was one pigeon that was very aggressive and tried to chase the others off the crumbs. For some reason the dominant pigeon made Stone think of Cardinal Giovani Donati.

"Palmisano here," said the *Gendarmeria* officer.

"Have you heard about the death of Cavallo?"

"Yes, I saw it on television this morning."

"Do you have any thoughts about it?"

"We have heard rumors that Ambrosiano Bank was in financial trouble. Only smoke and no fire, but I wouldn't be surprised if he wasn't stealing bank funds."

"So it looks like a suicide?"

"Undetermined, as far as I can see. The London police have listed the death as suspicious."

MURDER IN THE VATICAN

"But the newspaper said that he had a ton of money on him. That doesn't seem like a murder. Wouldn't a murderer take the money?"

"Perhaps, but if the Mafia was involved leaving the money is one of the ways they send a message. Like, he died *because* of the money. Something like that."

"Okay. That fits with some things I've been running across. I think there is some serious money shifting going on in the Vatican Bank and it seems that they are pretty much linked up somehow with Cavallo's bank."

"We see that linkage too, but financial shenanigans is a little out of our job description. I do know that Danilo Cavallo and Paul Sadowski were pretty tight friends. Cardinal Donati too."

MURDER IN THE VATICAN

"So it would seem that if this is a Mafia hit then the Ambrosiano Bank was somehow connected to the Underworld."

"And the Vatican Bank," added Palmisano.

"To the Mafia or to the Ambrosiano Bank."

"That is unclear, but look Stone – if you were going to launder Mafia funds you would do it through the Vatican Bank and not Ambrosiano Bank because it has to suffer visits by state auditors. The Vatican Bank has no such oversight."

"Isn't there some sort of internal oversight commission or committee?"

"Nominally there is. A German named Bernard Fertig used to head a three-Cardinal committee to oversee the handling of the money, but that was window dressing."

"Fertig is gone?"

"Deceased. That position is now held by Cardinal Giovani Donati. He heads up the AIF or *Autorità di Informazione Finanziaria*."

"Okay, I give. What's that?"

"The Vatican's financial supervisory body. Four Cardinals with Donati as the Chair."

"So if he has power and there is money laundering going on through the Vatican Bank then he and Sadowski probably know about it?"

"That would be a safe bet."

"What about betting that the Cardinal or Sadowski could be involved in the murder of Father Mendelsohn?"

MURDER IN THE VATICAN

"Less safe, but I know that worse things have happened in the Vatican throughout history."

"Yeah, I just finished reading Mendelsohn's book."

"I haven't read it," said Palmisano.

"Good read, but some bad doings in these old halls."

"I've seen some in my line of work here."

"Not a murder by a Cardinal?"

"No, not yet. Not that I know of anyway."

MURDER IN THE VATICAN

CHAPTER SIXTEEN

Colpo di fulmine. The thunderbolt, as Italians call it.
When love strikes someone like lightning, so
powerful and intense it can't be denied. It's beautiful
and messy, cracking a chest open and spilling their
soul out for the world to see. It turns a person inside
out, and there's no going back from it. Once the
thunderbolt hits, your life is irrevocably changed.
– J. M. Darhower, Sempre

Stone Harrison was still in the *Cortile della Biblioteca* and he had just clicked his mobile phone off when it rang. It startled him. He answered it, "Hello. This is Stone Harrison."

"Mr. Harrison I'm a reporter with *Il Messaggero*. We are one of the oldest newspapers in Rome. I'd like to meet with you, if you have time. My name is Fabiola Bellandi. I'm a senior reporter."

"How did you get my number?"

MURDER IN THE VATICAN

"Captain Palmisano gave it to me. He said you are working on the murder of Father Mendelsohn. Can we meet for lunch? My treat."

Stone glanced at his wristwatch. He saw that it was just after 11 o'clock. "Well, I have to eat," said Stone offhandedly.

"I'll take that as a yes Mr. Harrison."

"Call me Stone. It's shorter."

"And harder, but not harder."

She's witty, thought the detective. *I wonder what she looks like*?

****

When Stone got the answer to that query he was very pleasantly surprised. When he walked into *I Tre Pupazzi* he didn't know that it was a five star restaurant; nor did he know that

MURDER IN THE VATICAN

Signorina Bellandi would be so beautiful.

    The first thing he thought was that she looked like a "Bond Girl." She had long flaxen hair that hung down to her sprightly breasts and across her head she wore a wide black scarf tied off in a way that set her hair aglow. Her emerald eyes were mascaraed in black, which also set them off as dancing jewels. On her lower right lip was a small dark mole that gave character to her alabaster face.

    She wore a white blouse with black diamond-shaped onyx buttons down the front and on her right ring finger was a large black onyx ring from the Gatsby Collection, which had diamonds around the black gemstone Bezel-set. The diamonds were arrayed in a platinum bubble-like champagne configuration. Stone didn't know it, but the ring cost more than his automobile.

It was that expensively-ringed hand that the ravishing young woman extended to shake his beefy paw. She simply said, "I'm Fabiola. I'm glad you could come."

Stone Harrison was very glad he had. *What a knockout*, he thought. *Beats Lois Lane all over the place.*

It was an odd thing to think because at that very moment Fabiola Bellandi was sizing him up and placed his physique just slightly south of Superman.

Stone Harrison was six foot two and kept in shape. He had played Rugby, the rowdy type of football developed in the 19th century at Rugby School in Rugby, Warwickshire, England. Hence the game's name.

MURDER IN THE VATICAN

Stone said truthfully, "I'm glad I could make it."

They went through the normal "getting acquainted" talk and ordered drinks – a Baby Cham for Fabiola and for Stone a *Birra Messina,* one of the Italian beers he had not yet tried.

When they switched to business, Fabiola began, "My paper did a small piece on the murder of the young priest just after that unfortunate event, but because he was a well-known author I want to do a follow-up article on the investigation."

Stone took a long pull on his beer to gain time to think of how to respond. When he set down his pilsner he said, "It is not common for me to divulge details of an investigation. It is, as you undoubtedly know, still ongoing."

MURDER IN THE VATICAN

"I'm sorry to hear that. The Vatican is my beat, well all of Vatican City, that is. I would have hoped that you could give me something."

"I hope you don't think I came for a free lunch under false pretenses."

"A couple of lunches will not break the bank at *Il Messaggero.*" Fabiola stood up and pulled down her miniskirt and sat back down. Stone didn't quite know what that move meant.

Fabiola saw the look in his eyes and said, "The damn thing rides up and pinches me."

Stone just raised his eyebrows in response. He didn't know whether to believe her or not, but as far as he was concerned she could do that every quarter hour or so and it would be perfectly all right with him. He hoped she couldn't see how attracted to her he was. That would give her an awful advantage in their interactions. If they were going to have any beyond this luncheon.

In a matter-of-fact tone Fabiola asked, "Is there anything else interesting going on in that cloistered medieval world?"

"Like what?" parried the detective.

"Like some connection to the murder of Danilo Cavallo of Ambrosiano Bank."

"Why do you ask about him? He was not in the Vatican Curia."

"I have been watching him for years," the reporter said. "He is pretty cozy with some high-ranking officials in the Vatican, especially Sadowski over at the Vatican Bank and Cardinal Giovani Donati, who is supposed to be overseeing the bank."

MURDER IN THE VATICAN

She knows her stuff, thought Stone.

"Sorry to say, but I don't know anything about all of that, lied Stone, "I don't even know if Cavallo was murdered. He could have hung himself from that bridge."

In her mind Fabiola thought, *E sono sicuro che i maiali possono volare.* It was the familiar "and pigs can fly" retort. Instead of being openly cynical she shocked Stone by asking, "What about pedophiles in the Vatican?"

Stone drained his beer and signaled for another to buy time. Then he said, "Again, I'm just investigating a murder at the request of the Pope. I don't know much about the folks inside those walls – at least not yet." However, both knew that the media had been reporting on sexual abuses in the wider Catholic Church for years.

MURDER IN THE VATICAN

"And the wild parties with *Propaganda Due* members?" As she threw this dart in his direction she flashed one of the loveliest smiles Stone Harrison had ever seen on man, woman or beast. It had the intended effect – Stone was mollified so much that he returned the smile.

Given the media reports, it would not be out of the realm of reasonability to assume that the same behavior might exist within the walls of the Vatican.

When he composed himself by drinking more beer Stone replied, "You are asking me about things I don't know. I've only been at this for a short time."

Fabiola leaned forward conspiratorially and said, "Several members of the Vatican are secret and illegal members of P2 – that's short for *Propaganda Due*. It is a Masonic Lodge and it is forbidden to members of the Vatican hierarchy."

The detective wanted to turn the tables and thwart her questioning so he asked, "Can you tell me about this P2 and the parties?"

Just then the waiter came to take their orders and Fabiola ordered an Antipasto Salad with *Bocconcini* and Green-Olive *Tapenade*. Stone ordered the *Strozzapreti al Lardo di Colonnata e Pecorino di Fossa* even though he didn't know what it was. What it was turned out to be delicious, as well as expensive, but then the menu had no prices.

Fabiola Bellandi didn't mind. She was happy to gaze on Stone as he ate his pasta. Part of her brain was trying to figure out how to see him again.

In between bites of her salad Fabiola explained about *Propaganda*

MURDER IN THE VATICAN

Due and the Bunga Bunga parties. "We know about these parties because recently a prominent politician was caught at such an affair by the paparazzi and photographed with a known call girl."

"And clerics attend these parties?" asked Stone, somewhat incredulously.

"There are only rumors to that effect. The paparazzi have never been able to catch them on film. They don't wear their clerical habits, so it would be difficult to recognize a Bishop or Cardinal."

"Do you think that Father Mendelsohn might have uncovered this unseemly fact and been murdered to keep him quiet?" asked the detective, even though he thought such a question was a bit silly to ask. He was enjoying being with this girl and he didn't want it to end.

"I know very little about the priest or what he was doing at the Vatican. That's what I hoped to learn from you."

She hits that damn ball back into my side of the court awfully fast, thought Stone, as he pushed his empty plate away. "That was very delicious. A lot better than the food at the Vatican Cafeteria."

"I only ate their once," said Fabiola with a frown on her lovely face, but the frown made Stone notice her dark eyebrows. *Either she's not a natural blond or she darkens those eyebrows*, he thought.

He stares at me a lot. I think he likes me.

I shouldn't stare so much. She'll know that I find her fascinating.

174

MURDER IN THE VATICAN

While the food at *I Tre Pupazzi* was considered gourmet and among the best in Rome, its flavor was not what the two young people took away from the first meal together.

As they walked out of the restaurant two pairs of eyes followed them. They were the eyes of the men who had been hired to kill Stone Harrison.

MURDER IN THE VATICAN

CHAPTER SEVENTEEN

I don't know much about kisses, but I can assure you that hers were no less fierce than a swarm of bullets tearing the air.
– Xavier Velasco, Mexican Blogger

Stone Harrison had joined the St. Peter Fitness Club shortly after accepting the position offered by Pope Martin. It was close to Vatican City and Stone developed the habit of changing into his running suit in his apartment and running to and from the gym, working out on their exercise equipment, but showering at home.

To exercise Stone used an Abdominal Band Pistol Holster with a pouch for his Glock and two places for clips. He had never had to draw his weapon while running, or in the gym for that matter, but he didn't like to be without protection. That was one reason why he preferred to shower at home rather than in the health club.

He began his run thinking about the gorgeous reporter who had taken him to lunch. *I think she may have taken my heart*, he thought as he kicked his jog into a full run.

It had been a week since he met Fabiola Bellandi and try as he might, he couldn't get her out of his mind. *Was it her emerald eyes? Or was it her hourglass shape? Could it have been the lovely long blond hair?* Harrison couldn't decide, so he settled for thinking it was a combination of all those traits.

Well, she was also witty and a good conversationalist, was his last thought before he saw the Midnight Blue sedan pull around the corner directly in front of him. The window was down and since it was a crisply cold autumnal morning the detective thought an open window to be strange. It put him on alert.

When he saw the barrel of the Uzi his instincts took over and he rolled off the sidewalk to his left and onto the grass. He came up behind a Sycamore tree with his Glock in hand.

For a moment he thought it might have been a child's gun, but then the bark began to fly off the tree as the shooter let go with a full clip, 32 rounds. *That isn't a cap pistol*, thought Stone.

As the car proceeded along the street and the shooter was firing Stone stayed behind the tree and rotated his body to the left to keep the trunk between him and the Uzi.

When the car had sped off and there was no more firing Stone stepped out and tried to get the license plate number, but it had been covered with some kind of black tape.

From behind him Stone heard groaning and spun around to see a homeless man bleeding below the bench on which he had been sleeping. He did not have the benefit of the massively gnarly Sycamore tree and took several rounds from the drive-by shooter.

Stone ran to him and turned him face up, but the man had just taken his last breath and Stone heard his death rattle deep in his throat. CPR was not going to help this man. Stone took out his mobile phone and dialed 112 for the *Carabinieri*, the Italian police force. Had the man been alive he would have dialed 118 for medical emergencies, but the poor soul was gone.

MURDER IN THE VATICAN

It took the cops 13 minutes to get
to the park where Stone was sitting on
the bench waiting. He described the
shooting, the type and color of the car,
the fact that its license plate had been
purposefully obscured and most
dramatically that someone had emptied
a full clip from a machine gun at him.

The homeless man was a victim of
collateral damage, but it would not have
made any difference to him if the three
bullets that killed him were aimed at
him or were simply strays. Either way
he was given a three-pop pass out of this
world.

After the police released him
Stone continued his run to the exercise
club. He had been in shootouts before
and had even killed a man. This drive-
by was not pleasant, but he wasn't going
to let it ruin his morning workout.

MURDER IN THE VATICAN

Yet, while on the exercise bike, Stone began to wonder who wanted him dead and why? The why was the easier part. It had to be connected to his inquiries around the Vatican, but there were a number of characters that came to mind who could have been the shooter, although the actual man with the Uzi was most likely a hired gun.

Another worrying thought came into his mind: *Who else was at risk*? He had Marty Murphy working the case and Celso Palmisano had been consulting with him. Then he remembered the two men at the restaurant when he met with Fabiola. He hadn't given it much thought at the time because he was so enthralled with the exciting reporter, but thinking back on it he realized that he should have been more vigilant. *They definitely seemed to be looking our way a great deal. Shit! Is she now at risk?*

****

After his shower Stone found the business card Fabiola Bellandi had given him and dialed the number. She picked up on the second ring.

Stone said that he had to see her ASAP and would explain when they met. The detective suggested they meet at a pub away from the Vatican. Fabiola said there was one next to the newspaper – *L'Oasi della Birra* on the *Piazza Testaccio.*

"Two o'clock?'

"That's fine with me," replied Stone.

****

All the way to the *Piazza Testaccio* Stone was wondering if he was overreacting as an excuse to see *Signorina* Bellandi again.

Walking across the *Piazza Testaccio* Fabiola was wondering if the meeting was about work or something else. Her heart was opting for the "something else."

When they had their drinks Stone told her about the drive-by shooting, the death of the old man and how he was trying to put two and two together about the dramatic turn of events.

"Well, you are investigating a murder that took place in Vatican City. Somebody killed that priest and somebody probably hired him to do it."

"Most likely somebody in the Apostolic City," concurred Stone.

"Yes, it would seem to be likely and if they killed once, well ... ."

MURDER IN THE VATICAN

Stone took a drink of his beer, this time a new one – *Nastro Azzurro* – Blue Ribbon. "I could be next."

"It's a possibility." Fabiola was also drinking beer, having forgone the Baby Cham of their last meeting. Hers was a *Birra Moretti*.

Stone tried to change the subject and said, "I like this beer better than the *Birra Messina* I ordered last time."

She asked, "Have you tried this one?" Fabiola was drinking from the bottle and held it up for Stone to see.

"No, but maybe I'll order that one next."

"Try it first." She thrust the bottle toward him.

"You want my lips on your bottle? I don't think so."

Fabiola giggled and said quietly, "It's just like kissing."

MURDER IN THE VATICAN

Stone Harrison was fairly light skinned and he turned an indescribable shade of red, which Fabiola noticed and giggled some more. Then she deepened his redness when she asked, "Are you afraid of kissing me?"

When Stone gained some degree of composure he took the beer bottle and tasted its contents. "Good," he said, "better than mine. Ahh ... err ... about why I asked you to meet me."

"You wanted to tell me about the shooting before I read about it in my newspaper?"

"Well, that, but ... well, more than that. I think you may be at risk seeing me."

Fabiola let a wicked smile cross her lips. "I can take that one of two ways mister."

MURDER IN THE VATICAN

Stone got her innuendo. "Be serious. Somebody tried to kill me, most likely because of the Vatican case and they may go after anyone seen with me on a regular basis. Or you could get caught in a crossfire just like that poor bloke on the park bench." Stone glanced around the room, but did not see the two men that had shown excessive interest in them last time. He had given that more thought and was wondering if their stares weren't the result of Fabiola's beauty and not evil in a more sinister way.

"You're being a little dramatic Mr. Harrison."

"I told you to call me Stone."

"Stone's also being a little dramatic."

"Murder is a dramatic thing."

MURDER IN THE VATICAN

"But we ate lunch before and nothing happened. We're here drinking beer and nothing has happened. It will likely be like that if we get together again."

Stone stopped to think. This was all a bit confusing for him. He was no virgin, but he had spent most of his time working and only had an occasional affair, none of which stuck. He had decided that he was going to be a bachelor don like most of the old unmarried professors at Cambridge.

Fabiola noticed that the attractive man across from her was perturbed. She put her hand on his and said softly, "Were you wanting to see me for some reason other than the shooting? I was wanting to see you."

"You were?"

MURDER IN THE VATICAN

"I feel like we could be friends.
No, that's not true. More than friends."

"Really? You're not just saying
that to make me feel good?"

"If it makes you feel good then
that's wonderful, but I want you to know
that I have been thinking about you.
Have you been thinking about me?"

"Yes, all the time. I'm finding it
hard to concentrate on the case."

"Then we had better work
together on it. That way you can
concentrate and we will either fall in
love or come to hate each other."

"Can I choose which?"

"Of course."

"*Ho scelto l'amore.*"

"You have a heavy British accent."

"Did you understand what I said
with my bad Italian?"

MURDER IN THE VATICAN

"Anytime a man says he wants to love a woman it is not bad. *Baciami.*"

"I don't know that word."

"It means kiss me."

That's how the other side of their relationship started.

MURDER IN THE VATICAN

CHAPTER EIGHTEEN

The mind wears the colors of the soul, as a
valet those of his master.
– Anne Sophie Swetchine, Russian Mystic

Cardinal Nazario Viola was almost
as tall as Stone Harrison, which was tall
for an Italian of his generation. A man of
sixty-something Viola had a big frame
and a barrel chest, white hair cut short,
a strong broad face, a long slightly
hooked nose, flaring nostrils and a full
mouth. His eyes were intelligent and
sparkled when he talked, revealing a
man at peace with himself and his
position within the Vatican. He was
competent in his duties, but was not a
seeker of status or high station. Yet he
had achieved both.

Viola was the Vatican's Secretary
of State and the most important

MURDER IN THE VATICAN

Cardinal below the Pope in governing the Roman Curia, the administrative apparatus of the Holy See. The Curia was the central administrative apparatus through which the Pontiff conducted the affairs of State and the Holy Roman Church.

At Captain Palmisano's suggestion Stone Harrison made an appointment with Viola's secretary to meet with the busy Cardinal.

They met in a conference room with a rectangular teak table over an Indian rug, a gift from the mayor of Mumbai. The walls had the requisite religious photographs and a large wooden crucifix. On the table was a gilded gold clock, a matching crucifix on a pedestal and a gold pen and pencil set.

MURDER IN THE VATICAN

Cardinal Viola and the detective sat facing each other in padded straight-backed chairs.

Harrison explained that the head of the Vatican's *Gendarmerie* had suggested that they meet. Palmisano had told Stone that of all the Cardinals, Nazario Viola was the most responsible and honorable, a man to be trusted.

"I understand that the Pope has asked you to look into the unfortunate event regarding the young Father Mendelsohn," began the Cardinal. "How can I help you?"

"Captain Palmisano said that I could trust you and so I am going to try to be frank with you. I need your help understanding the structure and nature of the Vatican. Yes, I am to investigate the murder, but Pope Martin asked more of me. He wants me to ferret out any corruption as well. As you can image that is a tall order for an outsider. I need an insider's view on things."

Viola answered, "I have been in the Vatican most of my adult life and I am still trying to figure the place out, but I would be willing to share my views on things, if that would help you in your investigations."

"Okay, first question: are you aware of any financial misdealings?

"I have heard things."

"Such as?"

"One thing you must understand about this place is that there is an active rumor mill. Some facts get circulated, but they are leavened with many misconceptions and lies. I have only heard that the Vatican Bank may be pushing bad money through in order to clean it for outsiders. I believe they call it money laundering."

"Who do they do this for?"

"In Italy – who else? The Mafia. There may be others, but this is what I have heard."

"Who is doing this?"

"Those at the bank with the power."

"That would be Director Sadowski?"

"Among others."

"And those others are … ?"

"There is a committee that is charged with overseeing the bank's activities. One would suspect that they should know what is going on."

"That would be Cardinal Giovani Donati."

"Among others."

MURDER IN THE VATICAN

"That pretty much confirms what I have learned from other sources. What about sexual indiscretions."

"Bad behavior breeds bad behavior."

"Can you elaborate on that?"

"As you can understand Mr. Harrison, I am a Cardinal and in a position of great responsibility. I have to protect myself within the culture of the Vatican, which customs when violated can end a man's career here. I will help you with as much as I can, but there are others who know more than me and who are freer to speak of the kinds of things you wish to learn. As a general principle you should know that in the Vatican everything is intertwined and nothing happens in a vacuum."

"Who might that be?"

MURDER IN THE VATICAN

The Cardinal pushed his chair back from the table somewhat and clasped his hands across his body in a church steeple fashion, "I need to explain some things first. In the Vatican social structure there are formal and informal offices. Sometimes one can learn more from the informal folks than from those like myself who have to protect themselves."

"That seems reasonable based on my experience at Cambridge University."

"Ah yes, I would have thought that a great university like Cambridge is not very different in that regard from the Vatican."

"I see similarities, for sure."

"Anyway, perhaps the most important set of informal positions in the Vatican rests with the valets."

MURDER IN THE VATICAN

"The valets?"

"Each important position here has a valet attached. I have mine, as every other Cardinal does. Cardinals interact with each other largely at the official level, while their valets interrelate at another."

"They talk with each other, I suppose, just like porters in the colleges at Cambridge."

"Yes. The valet system provides the Vatican with a whispering gallery, as it were."

"A system of gossip."

"Which to you can be an invaluable source of information if you understand how it works."

"And how does it work?"

"There are levels of valets. The top level is the *Commendatore*. My valet is such, as are all valets of Cardinals."

MURDER IN THE VATICAN

"Does the Pope have a valet?"

"Yes, and he is a *Commedatore*, perhaps with a little more luster than the others, but of that high level."

"And below that?" asked Stone, as he was writing in his notebook.

"The next level down in the valet hierarchy is the *Professore*. He would serve Bishops and Monsignors mostly."

"What's the bottom level?"

"It's not exactly the bottom. There are the *Signores*, who take care of priests. Some non-religious functionaries in the Vatican's structure have valets that are not even *Signores*, but are simply referred to by their family names."

"It would seem that the valet structure more or less mirrors the religious hierarchy of those they serve."

MURDER IN THE VATICAN

"That is the case. Very perceptive. Furthermore, to know a Prelate's valet is the know the Prelate."

"I'm a little unclear about what a Prelate is?" said Stone, still writing furiously.

The Cardinal responded, "The Prelacy is simply a body of Prelates and Prelates govern. That governing could be in a diocese in Bolivia, for example. In the Vatican it is the same – Prelates are merely those who govern here."

"So I should talk to your valet."

"Among others." As that phrase kept coming up Stone saw his job getting more and more complicated. It would be a lot simpler, he thought, if there was just one good guy and one bad guy, but every time he found one there seemed to be "others" popping out of the medieval woodwork."

MURDER IN THE VATICAN

"What is the name of your valet?

"Fausto Massini, but let me tell you a bit more to help you understand the nature of a valet. These men are the keystones in our system. Through those they serve they know all the details of each officer in the Vatican's system. They know exactly how much wine is consumed, how much oil, cigarettes, alcohol, bread, vegetables, sugar, gas, cloth – how much of most everything – is used in the some 150 households in the Vatican. I preside over the official flow in information, but the valets know details about which I could never access officially."

"Tell me about your valet."

"Fausto Massini has been doing this his whole life. He started with me and is still my trusted servant. He organizes my life. Every morning he

MURDER IN THE VATICAN

wakes me at the right time for the day's events, shaves me, cuts my hair if needed, runs a bath for me, dresses me in the right clothing for the schedule ahead, makes breakfast, takes me to morning mass and drives me to any daily appointments I might have. What would I do without him?"

"He sounds like someone I should meet. When can that be arranged?"

"How about now? He is just outside the door."

Stone didn't know how the Cardinal summoned his valet, perhaps a hidden button under the table, but Fausto Massini opened the door and stepped forward, "You Eminence called?"

Cardinal Viola explained that he wanted Massini to help the detective and the valet nodded his head, "Now or should we set up an appointment."

"Now is good. I think I'll take a quick power nap. Sit down and talk with this gentleman, if you will."

"*Naturalmente Eminenza*," said the valet as he pulled the chair out for his master. "Would you like me to turn down your bed?"

"No, that's not necessary Fausto. Sit and speak with this detective. He is doing some important work here."

"I already know of his investigations, Your Eminence."

"I'm sure you do," said Cardinal Viola as he exited the conference room with a wry grin on his open face.

"How may I help you?" asked the valet. He had inherited a medium build, sloping shoulders, size 11 feet and a cultured way of speaking, which he

MURDER IN THE VATICAN

could do in five languages. He could cook, sew, do the marketing, vacuum and clean, drive, repair damn near anything, keep the books, handle the most delicate matters for the Cardinal, organize the correspondence and catalogue the many volumes in the Prelate's bookshelves. Like most other valets Fausto Massini took extreme pride in his position at the Vatican and held a serene, but ferocious dedication to his master.

Stone explained his charge from the Pope and brought him up to date on what he had so far discovered. "Can you expand on anything I have found or add anything regarding misdeeds in your world here?"

"You are on to some of it. Donati, Sadowski and the bank. There are things going on that surely could not be

203

considered normal banking procedures."

"But it is not a normal bank, is it? For example, they don't have state auditors come in. They are exempt from paying taxes. And probably other things I don't know about."

"Those things are part of their charter, but laundering money is not. Cavorting with criminals is not. Communicating with terrorists is not."

"Wait a minute. Did you say terrorists? What do you know on this? Is it just a rumor?"

"Everything I hear is a rumor Mr. Harrison."

"So what did you hear about terrorists?"

"There is a certain man who comes from London and then, after his visits, the bank receives boxes of cash marked as books. Sometimes it is different men from other cities. The pattern is always the same. He visits and then later boxes arrive addressed to the Vatican Bank. With London it's books, but other cities might have boxes labeled stationary or business cards, something like that. Sadowski's valet has seen this more than once. We put two and two together and think that the Vatican Bank is laundering terrorist money."

"I didn't mention this before, but we have heard from Interpol about this guy. See if you can get anything out of Sadowski's valet."

"I will when I see him. We have coffee together from time to time."

"What about sexual indiscretions?"

"They exist."

"Specifically."

"There are rumors of young boys, whores, wild parties. You should look into the Vatican connections with *Propaganda Due*."

"The Masons?"

"P2 holds *La Dolce Vida* parties four times a year. Some Prelates go."

"What do you mean by *La Dolce Vida*? It just means 'The Sweet Life.'"

"No, it is more than the literal meaning of the title, just as it meant more when Federico Fellini had Marcello Mastroianni riding on the back of Anita Ekberg at that party. It wasn't about horse riding."

"So what goes on at these P2 parties?"

"Valets don't get invited."

"What have you heard?"

MURDER IN THE VATICAN

"Just what I've told you. They are wild like in the movie, only real."

"Who from here goes?"

"The only two I know are Sadowski and Donati. There may be others."

They talked some more and then Stone thanked the valet for his frankness and help. Stone gave him his business card with his apartment number on the back. Fausto Massini promised to keep in touch.

MURDER IN THE VATICAN

CHAPTER NINETEEN

Don't shy away from confrontation.
– Pastor Sunday Adelaja

Cardinal Giovani Donati was not happy with the ongoing investigative efforts of Stone Harrison and called him into his office. The large man sat behind his desk in his red robe and crucifix necklace. He did not wear his bejeweled miter headdress.

"I've called you here today to protest your meddling in Vatican affairs."

"I am here at the request of Pope Martin, who outranks you by quite a bit, as I understand the Vatican hierarchy," countered the detective.

"That was to look into the murder of Father Mendelsohn, nothing more. Now I hear that you are poking into bank business and bank business is my business. Stay out of my bailiwick – got it."

"I believe that you have been misinformed Your Eminence. The Pontiff has asked me to also investigate any wrongdoing in the Vatican."

"Well you won't find any of that in the bank. I am head of the Vatican's financial supervisory body – the *Autorità di Informazione Finanziaria*. If there was anything untoward going on at the Vatican Bank I would know about it and put a stop to it." The Cardinal had a disingenuous smirk on his devious face. He looked like a Yorkshire Pig *aka* The Large White that hadn't been fed in a week.

"There is also the matter of your membership in *Propaganda Due*." Stone let that bombshell sit as if it had a burning fuse.

"What do you mean? That organization is off-limits to Vatican personnel."

"And several Prelates have crossed that line and I believe that my investigation shows that you are one of them. Do you deny that?"

"You sonofabitch. You dare to insult a Cardinal of the Mother Church? Where do you get off doing something so heinous? You are just an English professor or detective or whatever you really are. I think you need to go back to your little hole in the UK."

"I asked you if you deny belonging to the Masonic Lodge called P2 or *Propaganda Due.*"

"I don't have to answer your damn questions. You had better watch your step. I hear that you had a close call out jogging. You jog almost every day don't you? That can be a dangerous activity I hear."

"Are you threatening me?"

"I am warning you that there are thugs on the streets beyond the Vatican walls."

"Perhaps there are some inside too, the kind that hire those on the outside to do their dirty work."

"Get out of my office. If it were up to me you would be on the next plane to London, back where you came from."

Stone Harrison stood up. "Gladly, and as a point of fact the last man who threatened me got a one-way trip to Dante's Inferno. You might meet him there one day."

"Do I have to call a guard to throw you out, you impertinent bastard?"

MURDER IN THE VATICAN

    When the detective closed the office door behind him he had a large smile on his face. There appeared to be fumes coming from the head of Yorkshire Swine, like indications of deadly thoughts.

MURDER IN THE VATICAN

CHAPTER TWENTY

Whoever said money can't buy happiness didn't know about Harrods.
– London Shopper

London's *Page One Books* had watchers from Interpol and those watchers had watchers from ISIS, Hakim and Haifa Zaman. There was quite a bit of watching going on at 110 Charing Cross Road London WC2H 0DT. Down the way on this street in Soho was *Foyles Bookstore*. Nobody was watching it.

George Wolitzer had stationed two of his best men to keep an eye on *Page One Books*, which was open from nine to nine.

Special Agent Melvin Baker-Jones was sucking on one of the 234 cigarettes he would smoke on this stakeout while his partner Emily Proust was trying to

213

avoid the smoke as she peered through
the scope across Charing Cross Road at
the door of *Page One Books.*

She had cracked the window and
most of the smoke was being sucked out
by the rather stiff breeze in the Soho
District, the fashionable district of
upmarket restaurants and media offices,
though in times past it was a less
dignified part of London, housing, as it
did, many brothels and streetwalkers.

Across the street, above the
bookstore there was another flat. Both
Page One Books and the flat above were
formerly *Madam Molly's House of
Pleasure*, an establishment that
attracted all the best gents in London.

The flat was rented by ISIS under
the name of Benjamin Waters with a
different kind of sinning in mind. In it
were the two ISIS moles who had

migrated to London together 2 years prior, but who had never been given a task by Caliph Abu Bakr al Baghdadi until this assignment was cabled to them from Syria.

Hakim and Haifa Zaman, a husband and wife team, were tasked to stake out the bookstore. They were to watch to see if there were any police who had taken an interest in it, or in the owner, Anthony Aylmer.

Three days prior they had observed two plainclothes operatives set up a telescope across the street from the bookstore. It was aimed at the front door below.

Their instructions were clear. They were to insure that the currier with the ISIS money was to arrive safely and that no one was to interfere with the packaging of the money as books to be sent to the Vatican Bank.

Hakim had sent word to the Caliph about the development and received word back to watch those watching the store. If the other watchers tried to interfere with the currier in any way they were to be killed. Baghdadi emphasized that the money had to be protected at all costs.

Hakim and his wife were uneducated and he only had a menial job sweeping out the neighborhood Mosque. They lived on a stipend sent by ISIS, an investment that would be paid off if the couple was needed for any good purpose. That time arrived when the terrorists decided to send cash to Anthony Aylmer at *Page One*.

The Syrian couple peered across at the infidel watchers through a drawn curtain, taking turns every half hour. When she wasn't at the window Haifa Zaman tended a pot of Okra and Goat Stew on the stove in the flat's small kitchen, a Syrian recipe. The heavily spiced dish wafted through the rooms and gave the place the smell of home to the couple.

At the ready on a tripod was a Russian SVD sniper rifle replete with a Vortex Viper PST Rifle Scope. It did not make the place feel very homey. The muzzle had a Rugged Razor 7.62 noise suppressor that reduced the sound of firing to a quiet *Pfttt*. Hakim had never even fired the gun, which had been sent to them with the money for the apartment. He hoped that he wouldn't have to shoot it. He had it covered with a towel so they wouldn't have to look at it.

MURDER IN THE VATICAN

Two days after the Interpol watchers set up their telescope the currier arrived from Syria with the first delivery of cash. He was dressed in European clothes and carried a large Harrods' shopping bag. It contained one-tenth of the money that would eventually make up the book order sent to the *Ufficio Postale del Vaticano* – the Vatican Post Office, where it would be picked up by Bishop Sadowski and deposited in the Vatican Bank.

The currier, who was named Mohamed Sabbah, was a seedy looking man with straggly hair and a full beard. His eyebrows, black like his beard, were so bushy that you could barely see his dark eyes lurking beneath.

Mohamed had never been to the famed upscale department store, Harrods, on Brompton Road in

MURDER IN THE VATICAN

Knightsbridge. He bought the shopping bag in a second hand store in London's East End.

The Interpol watchers videotaped everyone who entered the store and that was no exception with Mohamed Sabbah, but the watchers took no special notice of him. He went in with the shopping bag and came out with it and another *Page One* shopping bag that presumably contained a book or books he had purchased. A foggy day when he had entered the store, it had begun to rain and Mohamed opened his umbrella and headed toward the Charing Cross tube station.

When Mohamed Sabbah came back the next day Emily Proust was at the window and just thought that he was returning one of the books and she didn't take notice of the fact that he again was totting the Harrods' bag and had no other bag with him.

On the third day Mohamed entered the bookstore when Emily had gone for some pastries and Baker-Jones was at the window and he had never seen Mohamed Sabbah before.

But on the fourth trip Mohamed made to the shop Emily was back at the window and she wondered why this same man with the same Harrods' shopping bag was back again.

"That's odd," she said aloud.

"What?" asked Melvin Baker-Jones, who was snuffing out a cigarette in the already full ashtray. It was so gross looking that it easily could have been photographed for an anti-smoking commercial to be aired on British television.

MURDER IN THE VATICAN

"That same guy has been here a couple of times before carrying a Harrods' shopping bag."

"Harrods? I saw him yesterday when you were out."

"Did he have that bag?" asked Emily.

"Yeah."

"Then that makes at least three trips. Something's fishy here."

"He has fish in the bag?" joked Baker-Jones.

"Don't try to be cute. This guy is not buying books and from the looks of him I doubt seriously if he's ever set foot in Harrods."

"Fish and Chips, maybe?"

"Stop it. This is important Melvin."

MURDER IN THE VATICAN

Baker-Jones lit another cigarette and made his way to the window. "Is he still inside?"

"Yes." Emily had the scope focused on the shop door. "Keep that damn cigarette away from me." Baker-Jones put it near the slit in the window to draw the smoke away from Emily. He liked her, but he didn't like her constant harping about his smoking.

When Mohamed Sabbah emerged he was carrying the Harrods' bag and quickly hurried down Charing Cross Road going toward the tube station.

Emily commented, "Multiple trips with a bag. The boss said we were to be especially alert for a delivery of the terrorist money, but what if this guy is bringing it in bits and pieces?"

"Could be."

MURDER IN THE VATICAN

Emily suggested, "Let's check the time stamps on the videos. If he comes more or less at the same time one of us should be waiting in the shop tomorrow."

The time stamps on the "Harrods Man," as they dubbed him, showed that he arrived at *Page One Books* shortly after 11 o'clock."

"The underground must drop him around the top of the hour and then he walks to the shop," reasoned Baker-Jones.

Emily said, "Tomorrow I'll be waiting inside and I'll try to get some close up photos of him."

****

The next day Emily was appearing to be browsing through the cookbooks when Mohamed Sabbah came in with a heavy Harrods's bag. He greeted the

MURDER IN THE VATICAN

man behind the counter. Anthony Aylmer took the bag and set it on the floor at his feet. He then took hold of a second Harrods' bag partly full of old books and put it back up on the counter.

"Have a good day," Aylmer said.

"You too," replied the currier and he turned and exited the store. Emily's camera was clicking the whole time and was positioned between Gisserot's *French Cooking* and James Beard's *American Cooking*.

When the currier left Emily noticed which two cookbooks she had moved to get her shots and thought, *I'll bet the French wouldn't like Beard's book to be that close to a "real" cookbook.*

****

Emily and Melvin reported to their boss at the London Interpol office,

MURDER IN THE VATICAN

George Wolitzer. "Do you want us to arrest the 'Harrods Man?'" asked Emily.

"On what charge – carrying a Harrods' shopping bag? We don't even know if this guy is ISIS."

"How do you want us to proceed tomorrow?" asked Baker-Jones.

"We need to find out what's in the bag. Is it the terrorist money?"

"What else could it be?" asked Emily.

"Drugs, pornography. It could be anything but cash," replied Wolitzer. "We better do a snatch. You both take up your posts tomorrow as usual and get the snatch on videotape. We want to see this guy's reaction when he loses the bag.

****

Shortly after 11 o'clock in the morning Mohamed Sabbah was heading through the fog for the bookstore when a motorcycle came roaring out of the mist and up onto the sidewalk. The passenger riding behind the cyclist deftly cut the cord on Mohamed's bag and snatched it all in one fell swoop. Before Mohamed knew what was up, the cycle was speeding down Charing Cross Road at top speed.

The Interpol watchers above saw the theft and got it on tape. As they continued to watch Mohamed stood dazed on the sidewalk three doors down from the bookstore. Because of the acute angle from their vantage point the ISIS pair in the flat above *Page One* did not see what had happened.

Haifa Zaman did wonder why both the watchers were at the window together and why they seemed to be intently looking at something down the street, but since she couldn't see she put it out of her mind.

****

Interpol Senior Agent George Wolitzer telephoned his folks at the flat, "Cash. Lots of it. We haven't counted it all yet, but it's in euros and dollars. Mr. Harrods Man is one of our terrorists for sure."

On the other end of the phone line Melvin asked, "What's next?"

"We wait and see if he comes back tomorrow with another bag of money. I don't know how ISIS operates, but if our Harrods Man was in the Mafia he may not be alive tomorrow. In any case, he's going to have some explaining to do about the loss of a lot of cash."

****

"We can't call him Harrods Man anymore," Emily said, watching

MURDER IN THE VATICAN

Mohamed Sabbah walk toward the bookstore.

"Why?" asked Melvin, as he approached the window to have a look. "Oh, I see."

The currier was now carrying the cash in a Marks & Spencer shopping bag.

"Marks & Spencer Man is a mouthful," joshed Melvin.

"We'll just call him 'Cash Man.' Tomorrow we get to play 'cops and robbers.' Whoopee!" Emily held up her hand for a high-five and Melvin slapped it with his nicotine-stained paw.

****

The following day Melvin and Emily were inside the bookstore appearing to be browsing customers and Agent Wolitzer and two other agents were in a car parked outside. London was cloudy with spitting rain, what Americans might just call a heavy mist.

When Mohamed Sabbah, formerly Harrods Man, entered *Page One Books* Wolitzer got out of the car and followed him in. The other two agents took up positions on either side of the door. Their job was to prevent anyone from escaping, but also to warn away any new customers.

Inside Mohamed set the shopping bag on the counter as he always did and Anthony Aylmer took it and set it behind the counter. That is when Agent Wolitzer drew his service revolver and announced that the jig was up. He actually said, "The jig is up." A fan of American gangster movies he had always wanted to say that.

Melvin had blocked the door and caught Mohamed who had tried to run.

MURDER IN THE VATICAN

Anthony Aylmer just looked like he had soiled himself.

None of this was observed by Hakim and Haifa Zaman upstairs who only realized that the two watchers had not shown up across the road at their usual time.

"Something is not right," surmised Hakim.

"Why?" asked his wife. Hakim opened the window and leaned out.

"We are not seeing the watchers across the street and there are strange men on the street now. Look. It seems that they are guarding the bookshop's door."

"They look like police," said Haifa.

"That's what I think."

"What do we do Hakim?"

The Muslim man stroked his beard to think. He didn't want to abandon his post prematurely, but it seemed to him that the police were not across the street anymore, but rather they were inside the bookstore.

After a few moments he said, "My wife, we go home. This is over, I'm afraid."

Afraid was not an idle word. Both Hakim and Haifa knew that ISIS might interpret this as a failure on their part. That might mean death for them, either quick or slow, but failure with ISIS meant death in some way or another. Death seemed to be the signature of ISIS.

****

The Interpol agents didn't get all of the ISIS money, but they got $4,883,652.00, which wasn't a bad haul, said Wolitzer, "That'll make for a nice Christmas party this year."

MURDER IN THE VATICAN

Anthony Aylmer and Mohamed Sabbah were arrested and deposited in cells in London's Belmarsh Prison, awaiting trials on charges of terrorism.

Interpol didn't know about Hakim and Haifa Zaman. They were chastised by al Baghdadi for not preventing the collapse of their plan and were told they would not be receiving any more funds from Syria.

Theirs was to be a slow death from poverty.

CHAPTER TWENTY-ONE

An eye for an eye will only make the whole world blind.
– Mahatma Gandhi

The ISIS Caliph, Abu Bakr al Baghdadi, was extremely unhappy with the arrest of Anthony Aylmer and the loss of money. He sent Farid Musab as an envoy to complain to Sadowski and Donati.

Essentially Farid Musab read the two Prelates the riot act and expressed the need for the Vatican Bank to cover their losses.

The Christians said that the arrest of the ISIS London contact was not their fault and therefore they were not in any way liable for the loss of the money.

MURDER IN THE VATICAN

Donati said emphatically, "That fiasco was your doing. ISIS bungled that bookstore drop, not us."

Farid Musab was enraged with the Christians and stormed out of Donati's office.

The confrontation was overheard by the valets of the Bishop and the Cardinal and word quickly spread through the valet network. They couldn't understand the string of invectives spewed out in Arabic, but they knew angry tones when they heard them.

Since Farid Musab arrived dressed in Middle Eastern robes and a headscarf it was apparent to all that he was a Muslim. He also had two Muslim bodyguards and a driver, all of whom were dressed in Islamic clothing and who, like Farid Musab himself, had full beards. They stood out like sore thumbs in the Vatican and they were noticed by more than one Mafioso while staying at the *Gran Meliá Rome Hotel,* which was only two doors down from *Don* Ganza's restaurant, the *Rinfresco a Domicilio Roma.*

"What are those ragheads doing visiting the Vatican?" asked Ganza of Lips Rotolo, his financial wizard.

Lucio Rotolo shrugged his shoulders and pursed his ample lips, but said: "Maybe they're doing the same thing we do over there. We clean our dough there." His cigar dangled precariously from his lips.

"Who are these guys? Oil sheiks have their own banks." Ganza was somewhat baffled.

MURDER IN THE VATICAN

"More likely they are terrorists with a need to launder money through the Vatican Bank," surmised Lips.

"*Al-Qaeda?*"

"No, they've been outclassed by this new bunch called ISIS or ISIL. Locals call them *Daesh*. They are much wealthier than *Al-Qaeda* or the other terrorist groups in the Middle East and the Levant. Since they generate lots of cash and need to buy arms, vehicles and all sorts of stuff on the world market, they need to convert the cash into digital money. Then they can send money anywhere in the world with the click of a mouse. The only way to do that is to deposit the cash in a reputable bank."

"Why use the Vatican Bank. For God's sake, it's a Christian bank. Why not some London bank?"

MURDER IN THE VATICAN

"They use the Vatican Bank for the same reason we do. Laundered money cannot be traced there because Cardinal Donati is the only authority with oversight and we keep him fat and happy."

"It's wrong to help the fucking terrorists. Bunch of camel jockeys!" Ganza saw himself as a good Catholic, even of the choirboy variety.

"These guys are more likely to ride around in bulletproof Mercedes these days. ISIS has billions of dollars at its disposal," said Lips.

"Whatever they use they are our enemies and I don't like Donati and Sadowski associating with such scum."

It was, of course, ironic that the Mafiosos were damning ISIS for doing more or less what they did. Both were guys who killed people for a living, but

MURDER IN THE VATICAN

in a sanctimonious way Ganza and
company felt superior for two reasons:
They were Italian and Christian,
although Ganza's participation in the
Catholic Church was limited to making a
yearly contribution to the little parish
where his mother had attended Mass on
a daily basis – his "sainted mother," as
the mobster thought of her.

"Maybe we need a sit down with
Donati."

"Good idea Lips. Set it up."

The cigar nodded, up and down.

****

Don Ganza was sitting in the
backseat of a black limousine. All the
back windows were darkened and
Ganza was dressed in a black suit with a
black shirt and no tie. It was black on
black on black.

MURDER IN THE VATICAN

The limousine was parked on *Via di Porta Cavalleggeri*, just off the south side of Vatican City. Donati in full Cardinal dress was a colorful contrast when he entered the limo.

"You wanted to speak with me *Don* Ganza?"

"Yeah and I want you to know that I'm pissed off." The Mafia boss was smoking a long cigar and he jabbed it in the Cardinal's face and a clump of whitish-gray ash fell on his red robe and he hurried to brush it off, lest it burn a hole.

"What's the problem?"

"You're cavorting with fucking terrorists, that's what's wrong. What the hell are you thinking dealing with these sand niggers?"

"Who told you this?"

MURDER IN THE VATICAN

"Nobody needs to tell me. I have eyes all over Rome. They came to visit you and they're still in the *Gran Meliá Rome Hotel.*

Cardinal Donati was silent for a few moments, trying to think how to appease the powerful Mafioso. Finally he pleaded, "Look, I don't like their ideas or practices, but it's business. Their money is as good as anybody else's money. They've got cash and they need to be able to write checks on a bank account. We launder the money and then send it over to Ambrosiano Bank. They have an account there and can draw off clean money."

"Christ man, I know how it works. We've been doing it for years, but that's not any excuse for dealing with such filth. They're not Christians, not Italians and barely human. I don't like it."

MURDER IN THE VATICAN

It was somewhat odd that gangsters like Servio Ganza would be so patriotic and so supportive of the Catholic Church. Yet Ganza was a fanatical nationalist. In fact, he had dreams of reviving Mussolini's National Fascist Party. He had been talking with his lieutenants about assassinating the Italian Prime Minister. Over the years he had been secretly infiltrating the army at the highest levels. A *coup d'état* would bring one of his Mafioso generals to power and the march back to a Fascist State would begin.

So far it was just a dream, but Ganza was less and less pleased with Carlo Prodi, the current Liberal Democrat serving as Prime Minister.

Donati decided to lie to appease Ganza. "Okay, they got their shipment of cash confiscated in London. Some fiasco with an Interpol bust on their currier."

"So what are they doing here now?"

"They're angry and want me to replace the lost money."

"Who lost it?"

"The currier and a bookstore owner in London. Well, they didn't exactly lose it. The cops took it in the bust." That

"That's not your fault."

"That's what I told them, but they are not happy about it. I don't think we'll be seeing the likes of them again at the Vatican." Donati knew that the ISIS leadership would get over the loss and be coming back for more laundering in the future, but he wasn't about to tell Ganza that.

MURDER IN THE VATICAN

"Fuck 'em. They got what they deserve. Goddamned butchers. I hear they go around cutting people's heads off with their sand nigger swords."

"They have videos to that effect," said Donati, trying to be agreeable. Since the back compartment of the limo was filling up with acrid cigar smoke the Cardinal was hoping Ganza was finished with him.

"Just be sure you don't see them again. If they want to come around here again, let me know. I'll have a little bullet party waiting for them – sort of 'lead *hors d'oeuvres,*' if you get my drift."

"I've got to go *Don* Ganza," said Donati as he opened the limousine door. Then as an afterthought he imprudently said, "Why don't you do the guys in the hotel in while you have them here?"

MURDER IN THE VATICAN

"Yeah, yeah. That would send a message back to wherever they came from, wouldn't it. Good one Donati. I'll do just that."

Cardinal Donati wasn't sure that would accomplish anything positive, but suggesting it made him look good in the eyes of a man who tended to solve problems at the end of a gun.

****

The next morning when Farid Musab got into the backseat of the rental car to head to the airport he was accompanied by his two armed guards. His driver held the door for him and then went around to start the car, which was parked in the underground lot of the hotel.

When the driver turned the key the Volvo S60 Inscription turned into a ball of flame, a firebomb that wound up

MURDER IN THE VATICAN

consuming nine nearby automobiles and setting off a three-alarm panic at the fire stations.

✳✳✳✳✳✳✳✳✳✳✳✳✳

When Caliph Abu Bakr al Baghdadi heard of the murders he was beside himself with rage. He suspected that the Christians at the Vatican were behind the bombing and vowed to send a suicide bomber to St. Peter's Square to mingle with the throng that always gathered there to see and hear the Pope on his balcony.

He told his lieutenants, "They killed four martyrs, but we will kill hundreds. I like that arithmetic."

Sitting on his rug the self-proclaimed Caliph began to ponder how the West had cheated Islam in so many ways and mathematics was one.

MURDER IN THE VATICAN

As an educated man, Caliph Abu Bakr al Baghdadi knew that Western scholars had tried hard to ignore Islamic contributions to mathematics. For example, in the African rainforest Belgian explorers found the "Ishango Bone." Scientists felt that the uniform scratches on it represent an Upper Paleolithic example of mathematical reasoning.

He also knew that most linguists traced the first serious use of math back to early Sumaria. But Caliph Abu Bakr al Baghdadi felt that the clay tablets showed simple counting, but true mathematical thinking was developed by Muslims.

There is some historical justification for this belief. For example, the word "algebra" comes from *Al-Jabr*, which is taken from the title of the

MURDER IN THE VATICAN

manuscript *Hisab Al-Jabr wal Muqabala* written by Muhammad ibn Musa al-Khwarizmi (780–850). He is today remembered in the widespread use of the term "algorithm." His invention of complex math was first introduced to Europe as a result of the translation of Khwarizmi's book into Latin by Robert Chester in 1143.

Caliph Abu Bakr al Baghdadi thought to himself, *When I take over the world for Allah I will rewrite history and our Muslim brothers of the past will finally get their due.*

MURDER IN THE VATICAN

CHAPTER TWENTY-ONE

But in the end one needs more courage to live than to kill himself.
– Albert Camus, Philosopher

There were nearly sixty thousand worshipers in St. Peter's Square for Easter Mass. Most were Christians, with a handful of secular tourists. There was only one Muslim and he was strapped with enough explosives to maim and kill hundreds in attendance.

He had been instructed to make his way to the front of the seating where the VIPs sat. He found this difficult because he had to push his way through the standing room only crowd at the back, then get through the seated throng in order to reach the small dais where religious leaders and government officials were sitting. There were also a couple of movie stars and popular singers.

To make his way through the crowd was made all the more difficult because of the bulky explosive vest he was wearing beneath his already hulking jacket.

It was a crisp spring day in Rome, but any observant security man should have questioned why this man was bundled up as if he was going on the Iditarod Sled Race in Alaska. Most such guards were too busy checking tickets and getting folks seated.

Eventually the bomber bent on martyrdom did manage to approach the dais just as the Pope was beginning the mass high on the balcony of St. Peter's Basilica.

MURDER IN THE VATICAN

Pope Martin was starting the mass with the words in Latin, "*In nomine Patris et Filii et Spiritus Sancti*," when the suicide bomber pressed the button. The blast transformed a religious mass into a different kind of mass – a mass of carnage.

Some survivors reported that the bomber had said just before igniting the explosives, "*Allah a akbar.*"

The Pope was quickly whisked to safety, but the bomb killed 328 people instantly, 183 more who died of their wounds in hospital and it maimed many hundreds more who survived, some with life-changing deformities.

Among the dignitaries were three Cardinals, an Archbishop, former Prime Minister Lamberto Amato and a visiting Russian Orthodox Bishop from St. Petersburg. The Italian movie star

MURDER IN THE VATICAN

Sophia Benigni and the famed opera singer Enrico Scacchi were killed as they sat on the dais.

Grotesquely, Scacci's head had been blown high into the air, while his upper body disintegrated into tiny bits of flesh and bone and his head came down to rest on the remaining hipbones of his lower body. It looked like his head was growing out of his pelvic area. His mouth was wide open as if he was singing one of his favorite arias. Very grotesque and very disconcerting.

When medical personnel got around to dealing with the grisly scene Enrico Scacci looked like a midget, although in life he was six foot four and a barrel-chested tenor. Three male and one female first responders fainted at the sight.

MURDER IN THE VATICAN

Most other victims near the bomb were simply blown into miniscule parts and strewn about and interspersed with the body parts of other attendees unlucky enough to be seated near the front. Bits of Bibles and Prayer Books were everywhere. One man was arrested for collecting bloody paper money and wallets. There were so many teeth on the ground that the medical personnel felt like they were walking on gravel.

The world was aghast at the heretical and blasphemous slaughter in such a sacred place.

Some thought that the bomber just selected St. Peter's Square because it gave him access to a multitude of victims and had nothing to do with killing Christians per se.

MURDER IN THE VATICAN

Others felt that it was an anti-Christian statement by Muslim terrorists. This view was given some credence when ISIS released a video claiming responsibility for the bombing and ending the press release by having the masked narrator shout: "Death to the infidels," in English and then in Arabic, "*Allah a akbar!*"

The story filled the news for weeks after the massacre. *Time Magazine* put out a special issue on the butchery. None, however, knew that ISIS leaders were targeting the Vatican because of the refusal of Vatican Bank officials to reimburse them for the loss of the money they had intended to launder through the Christian bank.

The secondary thing that rankled the ISIS leaders was the killing of their four Muslim brothers in the car

MURDER IN THE VATICAN

bombing. They decided a bombing deserved a bombing.

Perhaps had those facts come out, the story would have become much bigger and certainly more politically damaging to the public image of the Catholic Church. *Oculum pro oculo quem eruit* or بالعين العين – an eye for an eye.

Three weeks after the bombing ISIS released a second video showing the suicide bomber making his last declaration of fidelity to ISIS and Allah.

His name was given as Kosai al Refai and several members of the al Refai family were shown voicing their approval of the martyrdom of their relative.

MURDER IN THE VATICAN

CHAPTER TWENTY-TWO

When seeking revenge, dig two graves –
one for yourself.
– Douglas Horton, American Clergyman

Fabiola Bellandi and Stone Harrison had been spending a great deal of time together, some of it in bed, but most dining out, drinking in pubs and bars and taking tours through some of Rome's attractions – the Roman Coliseum, the Pantheon, the Roman Forum, the Catacombs and they loved to spend the warmer spring days sitting near Trivi Fountain and sometimes near the Spanish Steps.

It wasn't that Stone was shunning his duty as an investigator (*okay maybe a little,* he agreed in his mind) because he and Fabiola often discussed the Vatican case, but when the suicide bombing shook their world *that* came to dominate their discussions.

Fabiola said, "I've done some research into this bomber, Kosai al Refai. He seems like an unlikely candidate for *ifdshad*."

"You're showing off. What is *ifdshad*?"

"Martyrdom," Fabiola said in a self-satisfied tone.

"I knew that," lied Stone, grinning.

"Sure you did. Such a common and pleasant word."

"Why an unlikely candidate?" asked Stone, munching on a pastry while sitting on the side of the Trivi Fountain, a light mist wafting over the lovers, but it was a warm day and they didn't mind.

"Well, for one thing he had a bright future. He was studying

engineering at Damascus University. He
spoke fluent English as well as Arabic.
He was born 20 years ago in Allepo. He
was considered an articulate and
intelligent young man who did very well
in secondary school before gaining a
scholarship to the university.

"His father died when he was still
a baby and, for reasons that are not
totally clear, his mother abandoned him.
Kosai was left in the care of relatives
who raised him."

"Tough times for the kid," said
Stone, finishing up his pastry.

"Yeah, but on top of the loss of his
parents, Kosai experienced a second
more recent loss. He had fallen in love
with a militant girl who was apparently
killed while attempting to prepare a car
bomb. Kosai decided to avenge the
death of his beloved by carrying out a

suicide bombing. He conveyed a message to this effect to an ISIS man he knew and he was recruited to martyr himself."

"That all seems tragic, but so out of character for a young man with a bright future."

Fabiola continued, "Kosai had been radicalized in a Mosque where the Imam preached jihadism."

"Is jihadism a real word?" asked Stone sincerely.

"It is now. Follow along. Seemingly he began to read the *Qur'ān* intently as well as radical tracts. That's how he wound up in St. Peter's Square with dynamite strapped to his body."

"Why are you looking into all this?" asked her new admirer.

"The reason I research most things – a story to print."

MURDER IN THE VATICAN

"It will make compelling reading," said Stone as he picked a bit of pastry from his chin stubble. In the manner of the day, Stone wore a short growth of facial hair, sort of like he hadn't shaved in a few days, but he actually trimmed it almost daily to maintain the manly look.

"But wait – there's more."

"You sound like those television infomercials. Does the "more" come only with a small additional shipping charge?"

"You're in a goofy mood today" chided Fabiola.

"You mean this isn't a Disney movie – 'The Adventures of Donald Duck and Friends in Rome?'"

"You're making it worse Stone. No, I found a second video on an obscure Syrian website. It displays Mamoun Khauli, a young man about the age of the Vatican bomber. It shows his declaration of intent to commit *ifdshad.*"

"Martyrdom," said Stone, showing off his new knowledge of the term.

"Yes."

"Did it give any specific location?"

"No, but the scary thing is that in the video the young Syrian is not wearing traditional Arab clothing."

"Many young people in the Middle East dress in European clothes. That's not unusual."

Fabiola hesitated for a moment before replying. Then she looked Stone in the eyes and put her hand on his forearm, "But it *is* unusual for a self-proclaimed suicide bomber to be wearing a Christian priest's habit, replete with a dangling crucifix."

****

MURDER IN THE VATICAN

Fabiola Bellandi did some follow up work on Mamoun Khauli. She found him to be very different from the first bomber. Mamoun Khauli was not educated and was, in fact, illiterate. He could not even read the *Qur'ān* and he had to rely on recitings by his Imam at Friday prayers.

Mamoun Khauli did attend school, but it was a *madrassa* school where radical Islam was preached orally to young students from the lower classes in society. These propaganda schools were designed to turn out jihadist fighters and occasionally a suicide bomber.

Although some *madrassa* schools are not propagandistic, some are. An Islamic school of this type in ISIS-held territory offered a *hifz* course focusing on the memorization of the verses of the

MURDER IN THE VATICAN

Qur'ān. A person who was able to memorize the entire *Qur'ān* was referred to as a *hāfiz.*

The second course was the *ālim.* It was designed to produce Islamic scholars.

A normal *madrasa* curriculum included courses in Arabic, the language of the *Qur'ān* and Arabic *tafsir* or the interpretation of the scriptures. Students also learned *Sharia* Law and the *hadiths* or recorded sayings of the Prophet Muhammad.

Advanced students learned *mantiq* or logic, Muslim history and the history of ISIS. Much of the teaching in ISIS *madrasas* produced students who revered the accomplishments of the Arab world and denigrated those of the West.

MURDER IN THE VATICAN

Thanks to his *madrasa* training, Mamoun Khauli grew up to hate Jews, Christians and all infidels of the West. He knew very little about the distinctions between these cohorts, but his jihadist teachers stressed that it was their rejection of Allah and the teachings of the Prophet Mohamed that united them into one repulsive category – infidels.

When Fabiola told Stone about Mamoun Khauli he asked, "So they dress this kid up as a Catholic priest for the video – why?" Harrison thought he knew the answer, but he wanted to see if Fabiola concurred.

"I don't know, but I'm afraid I have a frightening theory?"

"That they plan a second Vatican bombing?" supplied Stone equably

MURDER IN THE VATICAN

"That's it. That's the thing that's been giving me nightmares."

"Here we are sitting in the lovely garden and you're having nightmares. And you're with a very handsome lover." Stone struggled hard to keep a straight face.

"With a huge ego apparently. You're right though, it is lovely here."

They were sitting on a bench in *Villa Borghese Gardens,* which was beautifully landscaped in the naturalistic fashion of an English manner. In the distance they could see the ornate *Galleria Borghese* with its great collections of paintings and sculpture.

"We can't predict when or where such a radical attack might take place love." Stone was trying hard to placate Fabiola who seemed to be obsessing on

the possibility of a second suicide
bomber.

"No, but if I was an ISIS planner I'd
be thinking about a papal mass that
would attract large crowds."

"Like what?"

"I'm thinking it could be at the
Angelus Mass in August in the *Basilica
Sancti Petri* – that's St. Peter's Basilica to
you."

Stone asked, "What is *Angelus*?
Why would that be a target more than
any other?"

"It draws large crowds. They
normally fill the basilica and folks often
spill out into the square and watch on
widescreen televisions."

"But what is *Angelus*?"

"It simply means 'angel' in Latin,
but the mass is a Catholic devotion
commemorating the Incarnation,

MURDER IN THE VATICAN

Divinity appearing the human form of Jesus Christ. His Incarnation is a central tenet of Christian doctrine proclaiming that God became flesh and blood, assumed a human nature and became a man who could die."

"Why is *Angelus* so popular?"

"It wasn't always so. Pope Gregory V started the rite with the text of *Regina Coeli* in 966 and it was performed off and on through the ages, but was revived in 1964 by Pope Paul VI. He began the public prayer on a weekly basis at St. Peter's Square accompanied by a short address to the assembled throng. It's one of the rites that attracts both devoted pilgrims and tourists. That's why I think it would be a perfect time and place for a second bomber."

MURDER IN THE VATICAN

Stone Harrison pulled out his meerschaum pipe and stroked it for a couple of minutes. Fabiola had learned of this strange habit and let him think. When he pocketed the pipe he said, "We need to alert the authorities on this. Interpol would be appropriate and any Anti-Terrorism Task Force with jurisdiction in Italy or Vatican City. I can coordinate with Captain Palmisano of the Vatican's *Gendarmerie.*"

Fabiola nodded. "You take care of that and I'll keep digging for more facts on this Mamoun Khauli."

Despite the beauty of the day and the lovely surroundings, neither of the two lovers was smiling when they parted.

CHAPTER TWENTY-THREE

There are decades where nothing happens; and then there are weeks where decades happen.
– Vladimir Ilich Lenin

Don Ganza of the Mafia was driving his Jaguar XJ along the Amalfi Coast. It was something he did from time to time to clear his head and gain some time to think.

The bombing at the Vatican had unnerved him. It had made him even more committed to resurrect Mussolini's Fascist State. He had been dreaming of becoming the new strong leader who could revitalize a decadent nation, a country that had been lured by the false god of democracy. *I would replace democracy with Fascism, the bringing together of all facets of society under my rule.*

MURDER IN THE VATICAN

His reasoning was that a strong central government was needed to fight off the ISIS threat and the major western powers seemed to be war weary and lacking the political will to take on the terrorists in a serious manner.

On that little automotive excursion the Mafia *Don* firmed it up in his mind. He was going to meet with his mole in the Italian army, the *Generale di Corpo d'Armata.* His name was LLario Forcella, the second highest-ranking general in the Italian army. He had to get the ball rolling. "It's time for another *Il Duce,*" he said aloud and laughed. Then he thought, *I'm just the man for the job. I can lick those ISIS bastards. The weak democracies sure aren't doing it.*

It was the kind of thinking that took him to the top of the Rome Mafia.

MURDER IN THE VATICAN

As Prime Minister, Ganza vowed in his mind to be a strongman like Mussolini.

****

General LLario Forcella met with Servio Ganza in the unofficial Mafia headquarters, the *Rinfresco a Domicilio Roma*. He was drinking Beluga vodka on the rocks and the Mafia *Don* was having a Campari, his usual.

Don Ganza was laying out his vision for the state once they pulled off a palace *putsch*. "We are in a position to change the history of Italy, my friend."

LLario Forcella knew that the *Don* had a tendency to be bombastic and he just nodded.

Ganza continued, "The glory of ancient Rome was captured in Mussolini's National Fascist Party. World War II ruined his chances to continue the work he had begun in building a strong military and a strong leadership. *Il Duce* was a strong man that is why our institutions were strong back then. We can strengthen them again and achieve that level of glory again.

General Forcella wondered how many Camparis the Mafioso had consumed before he arrived. "I understand your words Servio, but what can we do to make it all happen."

"We kill *Generale* Nolfi and the Prime Minister for starters. Then you and I take over the government and reestablish Fascism. Then we bundle all Italian institutions under our rule. That's the basic meaning of Fascism. It comes from the Latin *fascis* for bundle. We would control everything and therefore eliminate waste and avoid the paralyzing effects of a democracy."

MURDER IN THE VATICAN

The army man was taken aback.
He never dreamed that Ganza would go
that far. "Killing those men in the
modern world is going to have severe
international repercussions Servio.
Have you thought of that?"

"Have you noticed the
'repercussions' we are getting from ISIS?
So what if the President of the United
States and the British Prime Minister
wrinkle their noses at Italy for a while.
We will be strong and get stronger in
order to attack ISIS and put them down
like the dogs they are. We need to build
up our armed forces and send crack
troops to Syria and kill those bastards.
They are the infidels. They are of the
devil. We would have the true God
behind us!"

MURDER IN THE VATICAN

LLario Forcella could see that Ganza had his mind set. "How do we do it? The murders. Who do we kill first?"

"No, no. Remember Machiavelli – swift and brutal. We kill them both at once. On the same day, maybe even on the same hour. Then we take over the media and broadcast the news of our successful *coup d'état.* In his masterpiece, *The Prince,* Machiavelli advocated that violence must be done quickly and totally and only then can society move beyond the brutal events."

The army man had read *The Prince* by Niccolò Machiavelli like most men of his station in life, but he wondered if his ideas were not tied to more savage times in the past. He wasn't sure other European countries would stand idly by while Servio Ganza enthroned himself as *Il Duce.*

MURDER IN THE VATICAN

Nevertheless, he poured himself another expensive vodka and began planning two murders that would shake the world.

MURDER IN THE VATICAN

CHAPTER TWENTY-FOUR

*Italy, a land of great saints, poets, sailors, artists,
statesmen, businessmen, lawyers, intellectuals,
professors, journalists, whores, gangsters, religious
parasites and dickheads.*
– Carl Wm. Brown, *L'Italia in Breve*

Mamoun Khauli was summoned by Caliph Abu Bakr al Baghdadi.

"My son, you have been chosen for this great honor. Martyrdom for Allah and the glory of Mohamed his Messenger is the highest sacrifice, which will bring you the loftiest rewards in heaven."

"*Insha'Allah.*"

"Yes, all is at the will of God. And I have been called to send young men and women like yourself out to create havoc in the world of the infidels. With our bombings we are going to force them to

MURDER IN THE VATICAN

counterattack us and then we will
conquer them in the last great war on
earth – our Holy War."

"I am at your service Caliph."

"You are acting in the service of
Allah. I am just His humble servant. You
are going to go out among the infidels in
Rome and you must act like an infidel so
that they do not suspect you. With the
bombing at the Vatican the security
services will be on high alert."

"I will be careful Caliph."

"But you must create a camouflage
by breaking our rules. Allah permits
this to achieve a higher aim. You may
smoke and drink. You may visit the
Roman brothels. You will be given
plenty of money and you should appear
to be a wealthy Arab and buy lots of nice
things before you complete your
mission. Buy things that will be good for

your family. After you have made your sacrifice our people will retrieve them and give them to your relatives. Do you understand?"

"It will be difficult to act in this sinful manner, but I will do my best."

"*Insha'Allah.* Go in peace."

****

When Mamoun Khauli got settled into the *Gran Meliá Rome Hotel,* taking over their most expensive suite, his first dive into infidel pleasure was to order a bottle of whiskey from room service.

A first time drinker he did know how to drink like a gentleman so he overindulged and passed out on the divan while watching the Playboy channel on television.

The next morning he had a splitting headache, which he could vanquish by donning the vest and blowing himself into tiny fragments, but he wasn't scheduled to do that till the *Angelus* ritual at St. Peter's Basilica in a week's time.

Instead, he called room service for some Alka-Seltzer. He had one week to delve into the sin pits of Rome, but he decided he wasn't much of a drinker, so he decided to concentrate on whoring. That seemed a safer route. Even if he got a venereal disease it wouldn't matter. He would be in Paradise by the time the bacteria or viruses would have a chance to ravage his mortal body.

When he arrived at his first brothel the madam lined up a half dozen girls in various stages of undress and he was told to choose one.

He selected a strawberry blond that turned out to be a bottle blond when he got her completely undressed, but he wasn't going to complain about details.

He emptied himself into her twice and then paid a little extra for a full body massage, which was performed by another big buxom Norwegian gal who had hands like vice grips and attacked his body like she meant him harm, but the deep-body massage actually left him sated and sleepy. Big Bertha, as the whores called her, left him asleep on the bench.

When Mamoun Khauli awoke he selected another girl, this time a dark-skinned, dark-haired beauty and he paid for an all night affair with her, but his body let him down and in spite of himself he could not get an erection so he paid up and caught a cab back to his hotel. He still had six more days to live it up. And since he was young he figured

MURDER IN THE VATICAN

his body would rejuvenate with a good night's sleep and then he would get another prostitute to fuck, *Insha'Allah*.

MURDER IN THE VATICAN

CHAPTER TWENTY-FIVE

*Chaos is what we've lost touch with. This is why it is
given a bad name. It is feared by the dominant
archetype of our world, which is Ego, which clenches
because its existence is defined in terms of control.*
– Terence McKenna, Writer

Fabiola and Stone were in his hotel bed after an enjoyable session of lovemaking. She was smoking a Galois cigarette while Stone was at the mirror shaving.

"You should have done that before we made love. My face is all scratched up," she shouted into the bathroom.

His voice came back, "When I'm done shaving you can have me in smooth mode."

"Now you're bragging."

When Harrison came back into the bedroom he found Fabiola on the phone.

MURDER IN THE VATICAN

He hadn't heard her cell ring so he assumed that she had it on vibrate mode.

Fabiola was speaking in French, which he thought odd and it was a language he did not understand. When she clicked the flip-phone shut he asked, "Who was that?"

Gustav Holtz at the *Pan-European Anti-Terrorism Task Force.*"

"That's a mouthful."

"*PEATTF* is their acronym."

"Easier. Why were you talking to *Herr* Holtz. I assume he is German."

"Yes, he's the Director there and I called him about our bomber."

"Mamoun Khauli?"

"Yes. They have sources inside of ISIS and are aware that a second bomber is already in Rome."

MURDER IN THE VATICAN

Stone sat on the edge of the bed and tried hard not to look at Fabiola's pert breasts. He took out his meerschaum pipe and began to fiddle with it. "Look at the timing."

"Yeah, August and a week before the *Angelus* Mass."

"Do they know where he is in Rome?"

"No, but they are madly searching for him."

"Why were you calling the *PEATTF?*"

"Same answer as always – for a story I'm writing, but this one is more than that. We have to do everything in our power to stop this madman."

"He's not insane, but as a male suicide bomber he is probably mad as in 'angry at the world.' Most of them come from poor backgrounds and feel that

they have little to live for. Mr. Big in ISIS
offers them a chance to make a name for
themselves in the annals of ISIS history
and a trip to Paradise. As a sweetener,
sometimes they offer to provide the
remaining family a big payday. The ones
that come here with an explosive vest
have bought into that storyline."

Sympathetically Fabiola said
softly, "Anyway, I know you have your
assignment here at the Vatican, but I'm
going to spend some time trying to find
this guy before he is able to show up at
the *Angelus* Mass."

"Keep me posted and if you get
any hot leads, don't go it alone. Call me."

"I will Stone, but how about that
smooth cheek you mentioned."

"Are you saying I'm cheeky?"

"Come over here and I'll tell you
afterward."

MURDER IN THE VATICAN

The two lovers forgot about the *Pan-European Anti-Terrorism Task Force* or terrorist bombers. They had some "under the covers" investigating to do.

****

Cardinal Giovani Donati met with Franco Lombardi Lippi, the Worshipful Master of *Propaganda Due*. They were on a bench near the Armenian Memorial Cross in the Vatican Gardens. It was a place they felt safe to talk about the sensitive subject Donati had alluded to on the telephone.

"Did I interpret your rather obscure reference to mean that Ganza is getting political?"

"Yes. I had dinner with him yesterday and we both had quite a bit to drink and he started spouting off about how he had men in high places that could bring the government down."

285

MURDER IN THE VATICAN

"Why would he want to do that?" asked Lippi astonished.

"He has become obsessed with ISIS. He hinted that his men killed those four Muslims in that car bombing."

"Did he say that?"

"Not in so many words, but that was the impression he was trying to convey."

"The St. Peter's Square bombing must have pissed him off even more."

Donati lowered his voice, "You know Franco, I think he may feel a little responsible for that."

"For the suicide bombing? How so?"

"He said he thinks that was in retaliation for the car bomb that he had set."

Lippi inched a bit closer to Donati, "But Giovani, how does all that fit with

MURDER IN THE VATICAN

his claim that he's going to pull off a *putsch* of some sort? Is he losing it?"

"He's got guys in the army who are willing to back him on this. He went on and on about the glorious days of Mussolini and Fascism. He sees himself as a strong man like *Il Duce*."

"Good Lord," said Lippi in disbelief.

"Of course the reason I'm worried about this is that the fall of the Italian government would not be good for our investments. I have taken some church funds to build up various foreign companies and we are just about at a point where they are going to start showing a nice profit. If Prodi's centrist government falls we could hemorrhage money big time."

Two nuns walked by and the Cardinal and Lippi were silent till they

287

were out of earshot. Lippi asked, "What can we do to avert a political catastrophe?"

"It's the economic calamity I'm worried about. You know that Prodi is P2, of course."

"Yes, he has generations of Masons on his side. He rarely comes to lodge since he was made Prime Minister, but he pays his dues and will probably come again once he is out of office."

Donati asked conspiratorially, "Can you meet with him and appraise him of the situation with Ganza. We don't want this thing to go forward. Political instability would rock the markets and our investments could become worthless overnight."

Lippi nodded, "Let me do what I can. Prime Minister Prodi may already know about the plot."

MURDER IN THE VATICAN

"And then again, maybe not. I'm sure he will appreciate your effort in either case. You can gain some brownie points with him. That never hurts with a politician."

"I still can't believe that Ganza would be so foolish as to believe he could pull off a *coup d'état.*"

"He is a powerful man in the Underworld and maybe he wants to come out into the light of day. He has an ego about the size of the Sistine Chapel."

"More like St. Peter's Basilica, don't you think?"

Both men laughed nervously.

Philosophically Donati ended their conversation asking, "What was it that the 1st Baron Acton famously said?

"Absolute power corrupts absolutely."

MURDER IN THE VATICAN

Lippi laughed nervously, "It got Mussolini, didn't it?"

MURDER IN THE VATICAN

CHAPTER TWENTY-SIX

*While we are sleeping, two-thirds of the world is
plotting to do us in.*
– Dean Rusk, U.S. Secretary of State

Prime Minister Prodi did not
know of Ganza's plot to topple his
government and kill him. Even when
the Worshipful Master informed him of
this subterfuge, Prodi didn't believe it.

"Master Lippi, I am the Prime
Minister and well guarded everywhere I
go. Even if this fantastic plot were true,
even the Mafia would have a hard time
getting at me."

"Ganza is a powerful and crafty
man Prime Minister. I think you should
heed my warning."

"Sorry, but it just seems too far
fetched in this day and age. Jesus, this
isn't the 1960s United States of America.

MURDER IN THE VATICAN

It's 21st century Italy. I appreciate your coming to me with this and I will put my security personnel on alert, but I feel confident that we can handle anything that comes our way."

Prime Minister Prodi could not have been more wrong. Three days after Lippi's visit to *Palazzo Chigi*, the official residence of the Prime Minister of Italy, the General of the Army, Taachi Maderno, was gunned down as he was preparing to tee-off on the 17th green at the *Circolo del Golf di Roma*.

When the Prime Minister was informed of the murder the hairs on the back of his neck went up. He knew that the threat from Ganza was real and that he had to take drastic steps to rectify the situation.

What he didn't know was that his promotion of LLario Forcella to

MURDER IN THE VATICAN

Maderno's post was playing right into Ganza's hands. As yet, nobody knew that LLario Forcella was a Mafioso who had been cultivated in the armed forces for just such an occasion. If nothing else, Ganza was a farsighted planner.

Apparently he was both tough and clever. What he hadn't planned on, however, was that Prime Minister Prodi was forewarned of his plan to topple the government and moved quickly to have Ganza arrested and placed in solitary confinement in Rome's *Regina Coeli* prison.

Solitary confinement for Ganza meant that he did not have access to other prisoners, but guards did attend to him.

That was to his advantage. A guard who, for example, brought his food to his cell would hear a

293

conversation something like this: "I know your name. We know where you live. I know that you have a wife and two daughters. I know that you drink with friends at *L'Oasi della Birra.* I can have you all killed. Or ... ." And here *Don* Servio Ganza would pause of effect. "... or a large parcel of money will be placed in your mailbox. You choose."

Prison guards are not usually highly educated or intellectually astute, as say a college professor or a brain surgeon, but they are smart enough to make the right choice when given such options.

With a quarter of a million euros deposited in a numbered Swiss Bank account, Ganza's guard donned a full Medieval Monk's Cowl Hooded Robe given to the guard by Cardinal Donati and walked into the prison, apparently there to offer spiritual sustenance to the prisoners. The robe's hood prevented the other guards from recognizing their colleague.

Once at Ganza's cell the guard gave him the robes. They waited one hour and then hidden by the religious garb Servio Ganza simply walked out of the prison making the Sign of the Cross to each guard as he passed.

In case the ruse was exposed, Ganza also had had smuggled in an Uzi submachine pistol, which he kept hidden under his outfit.

The guard had on his normal uniform under the robes and finished his shift, left the premises and was never seen again. Even Ganza didn't know that he had moved to Switzerland and was enjoying his windfall.

MURDER IN THE VATICAN

Back on the outside, Ganza went into hiding at his getaway spot in the Roman countryside, *Villa Laurentia* that was part of a large farming estate named *Tenuta Santa Cristina*.

From that isolated and safe environment the Mafia *Capo di Capos* plotted the next phase of his takedown of Prodi's government.

MURDER IN THE VATICAN

CHAPTER TWENTY-SEVEN

He knows nothing; and he thinks he knows everything. That points clearly to a political career.
— George Bernard Shaw

Dressed in a stylish suit-dress favored by working women in Italy Fabiola Bellandi, the female reporter with *Il Messaggero,* managed to get an interview with Prime Minister Prodi regarding the murder of his top army general.

After waiting almost two hours in the ornately decorated waiting room of *Palazzo Chigi,* she was shone into Prodi's enormous office and seated in a 14th century French wingchair. She had grown tired of staring at cherubs and gargoyles and now she was in a room decorated in a Renaissance motif. There was a terracotta bust of Socrates by

MURDER IN THE VATICAN

Frenchman Charles Malaise on a pedestal in the corner, a reproduction of Rembrandt's 1642 *The Night Watch* and in the far corner there was a three-quarters reproduction of Auguste Rodin's *The Thinker*, in stone, not bronze like the original.

Prodi wasn't there and while sitting and waiting Fabiola thought it strange that the Italian Prime Minister did not have any Italian art in his office. After 20 minutes the diminutive Prime Minister made an appearance apologizing and citing affairs of State as an excuse. Fabiola thought his eyes were like those of a ferret.

"You're a reporter with *Il Messaggero.* I read it every day." This was a lie, but it was not the first the politician had ever told.

MURDER IN THE VATICAN

"I hope it's of service to you, Prime Minister."

"It is. It is. Now, I guess you are interested in the murder."

"We know the details – the golf course and so forth, but I would like to hear your opinion as to why someone would want to kill the top man in the military."

"We are unsure at this point. He did have a mistress and there is some speculation that his wife hired a hit man, but again that is just conjecture at this point." In fact, it was a fabricated story that Prodi's Press Secretary came up with to throw the press off the real reason, although Prodi didn't know the real reason. In fact, the General did not have a mistress, unlike Prodi and most other ministers in his administration.

MURDER IN THE VATICAN

He didn't even have a wife, as she had died of cancer three years before.

"The murder didn't seem to have any political ramifications because you were immediately able to promote General LLario Forcella to take his place."

"Forcella is a good man. Perfect for the job. The other officers all like and respect him. He will do us well in that position."

"Was the arrest of the Mafia boss connected in any way to the General's murder? It seemed to come right on the heals of his death."

"No, not at all," lied Prodi for the second time in a few minutes. We had been after Servio Ganza for a long time and it just so happened that our Anti-Mafia Task Force, the AMTF, located him and moved to arrest him."

MURDER IN THE VATICAN

Prime Minister Prodi was well aware that Ganza had escaped from Rome's *Regina Coeli* prison even though they had him in solitary confinement. It was suspected that a single prison guard had helped the Mafioso to escape by coming in dressed as a visiting priest and then giving the robes to Ganza who left the prison easily because the guards merely thought it was the priest leaving after meeting with prisoners.

Ganza's whereabouts were not known to the police and they were misleadingly appearing to look for him, although the Mafia boss had enough of them on his payroll that the officers never went near his villa.

Fabiola asked the Prime Minister a series of stock questions about his hopes for the future of his party, Italy in general and the European Union more broadly.

Then they moved on to discuss international affairs, especially the threat to western civilization from ISIS and other terrorist groups.

Prodi pontificated, "I feel quite confident that working with the American President to take a measured approach to ISIS is the correct strategy. We certainly don't want boots on the ground, now do we?"

Fabiola demurred, "Prime Minister, it would seem that your so-called 'measured approach' is a measure or two short of the mark. We may need to send troops to Syria to clean up that mess."

Prodi laughed, "I can see that you will never be a politician. Sending

MURDER IN THE VATICAN

troops would be political suicide for me and my administration."

Fabiola didn't want to get into a pissing match with the man, so she merely said that she hoped his approach would work out in the end. Privately she thought that Prodi was more interested in hanging onto power than solving the problem.

The reporter thanked the Italian Prime Minister for his time, shook his hand and left the *Palazzo Chigi*, the building of which had been completed in 1580.

Outside she made her way to the *Piazza Colonna* where she had planned to meet her paper's photographer at the Column of Marcus Aurelius. He had been taking pictures of the palace of the Prime Minister for the article.

MURDER IN THE VATICAN

Together they hailed a cab and
returned to the offices of *Il Messaggero.*

MURDER IN THE VATICAN

CHAPTER TWENTY-EIGHT

*To me, the thing that is worse than death is betrayal.
You see, I could conceive death, but I could not
conceive betrayal.*
— Malcolm X

Don Servio Ganza met with
General LLario Forcella and together
they planned a meeting at the villa of all
the major army brass, those who could
aid in a palace *putsch* and those who
would oppose such a move. It was a
gathering to separate the sheep from the
wolves. Ganza wasn't interested in
having sheep in his administration.

There were some 26 officers
seated in folding chairs on Ganza's
massive patio by a heart-shaped pool.
There was plenty of finger food and
alcohol for the attendees and the mood
was upbeat as they had been promised

MURDER IN THE VATICAN

an evening Bunga Bunga party. None of
the officers wore their uniforms and in
the warm summer afternoon some were
in swimming trunks.

Ganza had installed a PA system
and LLario Forcella strode up to the
podium and tapped it to see if it was
working. There was a loud crack and
seeing that it was in working order he
began, "Gentlemen, welcome to our little
get together."

He went on to praise those
present on a good year in the corps and
stated that he hoped they could
continue the fine work begun by his
predecessor, who had so tragically been
taken from them.

Those in the audience did not
know that the General had been
murdered at the behest of the speaker
and Servio Ganza who sat off to the side

of the podium. Few knew who the Mafioso really was, but it was apparent to most that this was his villa and he and LLario Forcella were tight.

Then the new head of the army dropped a bombshell on the group. He explained that he was planning a *coup d'état* to oust the administration of Prime Minister Carlo Prodi.

A nervous murmur went through the men. Some squirmed in their seats. One officer in the back stood up and looked as if he wanted to leave. Another somewhere in the crowd muttered, "Oh no!"

Forcella went on to explain that the threat from terrorists was not being met adequately by western powers and Prodi's centrist party had been particularly slow to offer any credible resistance to ISIS and the *Al-Qaeda*, among others.

"This has to stop. Most of us here agree to that premise. We must defeat ISIS and the other threats. But how? Will Prodi's lackeys do that?

Several officers shouted "no!"

Ganza saw that the momentum was picking up.

"If the *Partido Centro Democratico* won't do it, then we must look to what has been successful in the past and that success shines brightest in the monumental achievements of Benito Mussolini's National Fascist Party."

A collective gasp could be heard from the crowd.

"*Il Duce* was a forceful leader. We need strong leadership. I am going to put in a man who is the *Duce* of the future, the man who will cut off the head

MURDER IN THE VATICAN

of Caliph Abu Bakr al Baghdadi and
bring down his evil quasi-religious
organization. I give you Servio Ganza."

The Mafia leader rose to his feet
and LLario Forcella began to clap. His
lead was followed by about a third of the
men in the audience.

Ganza slowly made his way to the
rostrum. He stood there for five
minutes looking at the crowd. Many
were ill at ease with this silence and a
nervous shudder went through the
throng like tidal wave.

Then, suddenly and without
warning, Ganza raised his hand in a
fascist salute and shouted at the top of
his lungs, "*Forza*! – strength!"

Then, "*Potenza*! – power!" even
louder.

Then again, "*Resistenza*! –
resistance!"

MURDER IN THE VATICAN

After that he was again silent,
surveying the crowd, taking its
emotional pulse. Then quietly in a small
voice that could barely be heard he said,
"*E la vittoria* – And victory." Then a little
after that, "*Per la Patria* – For the
Fatherland."

The men in the crowd leaned
forward to hear what Ganza was saying.
Some asked those next to them for
clarification. Ganza had their full
attention.

It was a masterful performance
modeled after the oratory of Hitler and
Mussolini. It had the same effect of
stirring patriotic emotions in most of
those present. Some stood and
applauded. Others clapped from their
seats. A few dissenters weren't sure
what to do. They had come thinking this

was to be a happy affair and now this shocker.

Ganza went on in a normal voice. "General Forcella and I want to let anyone who cannot support this movement to feel free to leave. I have valets who will bring your cars around. Those who feel that they cannot support my takeover of the Italian government please leave so we can continue with our rally. *Italia per sempre* – Italy forever!"

At first only three men headed for the parking lot where the valets were waiting. Then within a matter of minutes a cluster of eight men stood waiting for their cars.

As it turned out, they would not drive away because the valets were Mafioso and began shooting the unarmed soldiers. In less than a minute all eight lay bleeding on the pavement.

From the patio the rest of the officers heard and saw the slaughter.

Ganza said, "Are there any more dissenters?"

The crowd was silent.

"Bravo. I will turn the meeting back over to General Forcella who will give you the details of how you are to aid in the takeover of Prodi's effete government."

LLario Forcella stepped again to the rostrum and laid out a well-designed plan to oust the government. He did not mention that it included killing Carlo Prodi, the country's top leader.

In the news media the next day it was announced that eight top army officers attending a party had been too intoxicated to drive and while being driven to their homes in a van all were killed and burned as the van went off an embankment and burst into flames. The article went on to list their names and ranks in the armed services.

CHAPTER TWENTY-NINE

*Every leader, and every regime, and every movement,
and every organization that steps across the line to
terrorism must be banished from the discourse of
civilized human life.*
— Alan Keyes, Author

Late into the evening Prime Minister Prodi was in his office reading about the tragic deaths of eight top military men when there was a knock on the door. He thought it a bit strange as his staff had all long ago gone home.

"*Inserire* – Come in."

The door opened slowly to reveal a cleaning man with a broom and a cart. He pushed his cart inside and made like he was about to sweep the floor.

"I'm still working. Can you clean the other offices before this one? I'll only be another 20 minutes or so."

MURDER IN THE VATICAN

The cleaner nodded, but stepped close to the Prime Minister and jabbed him with the end of his broom handle. It had a hypodermic needle designed to extend under pressure releasing its deadly dose of Phenol into the victim.

The Prime Minister looked startled, dropped his newspaper and started to stand up. "What the f ... ?" The politician came close to dying with an explicative on his lips, but he dropped dead on his office floor before he could get the swear word out.

Prodi had been injected with a deadly toxin that affects the central nervous system, causes sudden collapse of all vital organs and a loss of consciousness. Death follows severe cramping as the motor activity controlled by the central nervous system shuts down.

MURDER IN THE VATICAN

This was the same lethal poison used by Nazi doctors during World War II. They injected thousands of prisoners with a gram of Phenol, a dose sufficient to cause death in the average sized human. Prodi received three grams. It took him three minutes and 14 seconds to die, but he was lucky to be unconscious almost instantly.

Prodi didn't know he was dying, nor did he know that he was the victim of a *coup d'état* that would topple his government and usher in a new Fascist Era – the Ganza Era.

****

The next morning General LLario Forcella announced that the Prime Minister had been murdered and the few remaining workers at the *Palazzo Chigi* had reported seeing a man fleeing the building dressed in an Islamic gown and a headdress of Middle Eastern origin. Of course, this was untrue, but it was part of Ganza's plan to confuse the public during the transition period.

Next, General Forcella sent one group of his trusted officers to corral the lawmakers in the *Parlamento Italiano.* The Italian soldiers were not wearing their army uniforms, however. Instead they wore Islamic clothing to make the terrorist attack on the parliament look like terrorism.

It was a bloodbath. Using automatic weapons, grenades and gas bombs they killed all 630 *deputati* of the Chamber of Deputies as well as the 315 *senatori* of the Senate.

Other groups of soldiers were sent to secure all radio and television stations. Each began to broadcast a set message announcing that the General of

the Army was forming a new interim
government due to a massive loss of
lawmakers and political leaders due to
an ISIS attack.

The international press said that
the attack on the Italian parliament was
the most heinous since the Paris
bombings.

The Italian public could not watch
their favorite *telenovelas* or their
sitcoms. Every radio station and TV
channel had the same repetitive
message – "A new strong government is
taking shape to save Italy from terrorist
insanity. Wait for the appearance of our
new *Duce*."

At the bottom of each television
screen ran a written message strip
saying in bold letters:

MURDER IN THE VATICAN

FASCISM IS BACK TO SAVE OUR
SACRED COUNTRY. *LUNGA VITA IL
DUCE* – LONG LIVE THE LEADER.

CHAPTER THIRTY

*You must have chaos within you to give birth to a
dancing star.*
— Friedrich Nietzsche

Pope Martin called Stone Harrison
to his quarters in the Vatican. The Pope,
like the civilized world at large, was
shocked by the brutal takedown of the
Prodi government and the ascendency
of an unknown fascist at the head of the
government, backed apparently, by a
military *putsch*.

"Mr. Harrison. I know that you
have been doing what I instructed you
to do, but in light of the terrible events
of the recent past and the apparent rise
of the ugly head of Fascism again in
Italy, something I never thought could
happen again I might say, I would like to
know if you have any information that

MURDER IN THE VATICAN

would indicate that anyone in the Vatican was involved in the plot to take over the Prodi government." The Pope's voice was weak and he was outwardly very shaken by the events.

"No Your Eminence. None. There are some sinful things going on, it would seem, and some unseemly characters at work, but nothing on the scale of revolution or terrorism."

"Of course, that is a good news/bad news report, but at least I am happy to know that the Vatican stands apart from these terrible doings."

Cautioning the Pope, Stone said, "Yet, just because I have not heard anything does not mean that nothing exists. Let me plug into the best network I know in the Vatican to find out if anything is amiss in this regard. I am referring to the web of valets. If anyone knows they will know. They are the tape recorders of the Vatican."

"I would appreciate if you could spend some time on this. I also want you to know that I stand firm against Fascism. I plan to make that clear in a papal address to the world."

Harrison said, "It is a confusing time Your Eminence. And I don't think we know exactly what happened, especially at the parliament building. I have a reporter friend who is convinced that those men dressed as Islamic terrorists were trying to deceive the public."

"Why would they do that?"

"In his address to the nation General LLario Forcella said that one reason the armed forces were moving to take over the government was to fight the ISIS terrorists who had killed so many of Italy's politicians. He linked this to the suicide bombing here at the Vatican. That's a neat package of linkages, but my newspaper friend doesn't buy it. Neither do I."

"Does the General want to become the Prime Minister?"

"No. It seemed he is promoting a shady character called Servio Ganza as the new Mussolini – *Il Duce*. You may not have heard this morning's broadcast."

"No, I was in morning Mass."

"Forcella said that this Servio Ganza is a strong man like Mussolini was and that this is precisely what the nation needs in light of the terrorist threat from ISIS."

"Something is rotten and it's not in Denmark," said the Pontiff, paraphrasing Marcellus' line in Shakespeare's *Hamlet*.

MURDER IN THE VATICAN

"We will learn more as things settle in. My newspaper friend and most reporters at her paper are spending a great deal of time and effort to get to the bottom of things. Who is this Servio Ganza and why is LLario Forcella pushing him forward as Italy's savior?"

"In any case, I am coming out against Fascism as a point of Christian principle. I want to put the moral force of the Catholic Church out there as being most ardently against totalitarianism. Fascism is just another form of the ideology being espoused by ISIS."

"I agree. Their ideology is totalitarian though they claim to have God behind them."

"We Christians made that same mistake in the Crusades, as you may recall."

MURDER IN THE VATICAN

"And Mussolini's Fascism was simply totalitarianism without the God factor."

The Pope said, "*Il Duce* claimed to be a Christian, but I think that was window dressing. Mussolini deemed it necessary for Italy to assert its superiority and strength and to avoid succumbing to decay. Now the justification seems to be ISIS – the need to defend Italy against terrorism."

"It may be a fabricated end to justify the means."

"In any case Mr. Harrison, check with your sources here in our little world. I want to be absolutely sure that the Vatican is blameless in this shameless takeover of an elected government. I am working on the text of my speech and when it is finished I will announce to the world my opposition to

MURDER IN THE VATICAN

Fascism in whatever form it rears its ugly head."

****

Cardinal Donati heard of the conversation between the Pope and the detective from the Pope's Secretary, Monsignor Alfio Corvi while both were attending a *Propaganda Due* conclave.

Corvi said, "The Pope is preparing a major speech to condemn this military *coup d'état* and the fascist ideas the new government seems to be promoting. I thought you should know."

"I am grateful to you Monsignor. I remember my friends."

Corvi knew that Donati was a power within the Vatican. He knew that there was a new road opening, a fresh pathway to power. He wanted to be part of that since he felt that Pope Martin's health was faltering.

MURDER IN THE VATICAN

Monsignor Corvi didn't want to be left out of the next regime in the Vatican.

****

Cardinal Donati visited *Don* Servio Ganza at his villa to inform him of the Pope's position against him and the new government. After a lengthy discussion of the implications of a the Pontiff coming out against the Ganza government the new *Duce* gave the Cardinal his instructions, "That Papal announcement should not take place. See to it."

Donati knew that when the Mafia *Don* and new Mussolini gave an order, it was unwise not to carry it out. Behind each command was an implicit threat of bodily harm or death.

MURDER IN THE VATICAN

CHAPTER THIRTY-ONE

He who seeks to deceive will always find someone
who will allow himself to be deceived.
— Niccolò Machiavelli, *The Prince*

Pope Martin cancelled the *Angelus* Mass until further notice due to the chaos in the country following the murder of the Prime Minister and the military *coup d'état*.

This threw a very large wrench in the plans of ISIS to carry out another suicide bombing. It also threw the second bomber Mamoun Khauli into limbo. He continued to enjoy the sinful pleasures of Rome and waited for further instructions from Caliph Abu Bakr al Baghdadi.

Yet Khauli was not altogether unhappy with the delay. He was, for the first time in his life, enjoying himself and

MURDER IN THE VATICAN

he was coming to see Western life in a very different light that it had been portrayed to him in the Madrasa schools. Second thoughts about killing himself for the ISIS cause were beginning to form in his young mind.

Stone Harrison too was relieved by this postponement because it gave him and Fabiola more time to find a way to prevent a second bombing.

Stone did as the Pontiff had instructed him to do and mined the valet network to see if anyone in the Vatican had knowledge of the fascist plot or if any Vatican personnel were involved more deeply in it.

His mining paid off. The valets indicated that there were rumors that Cardinal Donati had connections to the man General LLario Forcella was putting forward as the next *Duce*.

MURDER IN THE VATICAN

"Mind you, these are just rumors," cautioned Fausto Massini, the valet to whom Harrison was most close.

"Is this something new?" asked the detective.

"No, Donati has seen him before. They both are members of *Propaganda Due*. But maybe the political thing is new. Nobody could have seen the *putsch* coming and I never heard anyone mention that Servio Ganza was anything more than a big time thug in the Underworld."

Harrison thought to himself, *Now he's a big thug on a larger stage.*

Stone and Fabiola were as shocked as anyone at the carnage at the Italian payment building and the murder of the Prime Minister. It made headlines all around the world and the talking heads, especially in the United

MURDER IN THE VATICAN

States, finally had some gritty material on which to gnash their teeth.

Then it just died down and fell off the media wires. An ISIS bombing at the Super Bowl in the United States shoved the Italian *putsch* to the margins. Good papers like *The New York Times* and London's *The Guardian* still ran stories on the *putsch*, but they were buried deep in the back pages of the international news sections.

"They really pulled off a Machiavellian feat, didn't they?" said Fabiola.

"Reading *The Prince* in college was a real eye-opener for me. I even memorized some Machiavelli's more pithy sayings."

"Such as?"

"Let me see ... oh yeah, here's one I still remember: 'It is much safer to be

MURDER IN THE VATICAN

feared than loved because love is
preserved by the link of obligation
which, owing to the baseness of men, is
broken at every opportunity for their
advantage; but fear preserves you by a
dread of punishment which never fails.'"

"That's what the murderers were
trying to do. I don't buy the terrorist
angle, do you?"

"No, I think whoever killed Prodi
wanted other politicians of that ilk to
disappear from the political scene.
Without them the revolutionaries would
have a more or less blank slate on which
to write their new laws."

****

Monsignor Alfio Corvi, Secretary
to Pope Martin, wasn't especially happy
about the task that *Don* Servio Ganza
had set for him. What he was about to
do went way beyond a simple

MURDER IN THE VATICAN

misdemeanor. Ganza had tasked him to kill his boss – Pope Martin VI.

Ganza said, "Here is the address of the store where you can get it. I phoned ahead and they're expecting you."

Corvi asked, "Isn't it dangerous – I mean to me?"

"It comes in a sealed box especially made for snakes."

They were talking about the Death Adder, a lethal serpent with highly toxic venom that would kill a person quickly by shutting down the nervous system.

Corvi made his way to the address on the card, which was that of *Flavio's Pet Store* – "Come and Pet our Pets." Since Flavio sold deadly snakes his street address seemed appropriate: *666*

MURDER IN THE VATICAN

Via della Divina Provvidenza – 666
Divine Providence Street.

Flavio instructed Monsignor Corvi, who was dressed in civilian clothes, on the proper handling of the snake container. "When you want the snake to come out just undo the latch at the top and step back. It will push its way out and begin to roam in search of a warm-blooded animal to bite."

Flavio thought that the secretary was going to let the Death Adder loose on a rat or mouse, its normal food source. He had no idea of the dastardly deed the snake would bring off within the walls of the Vatican.

The Death Adder would kill a rodent in seconds, but it would take the Pope about a quarter of an hour to die, although he would probably be in a coma for most of that time.

Corvi had some misgivings about his task, but *Don* Ganza had mentioned that there were many new positions opening up in the new government and also new ecclesiastical openings would be made by the Pope's demise. Greed won the day over conscience.

****

After the Pope had been in his bed for something less than an hour Corvi quietly opened the door to his bedroom and stepped inside. The room was dark, but the Monsignor could hear the deep breathing of the Pontiff across the room.

Corvi walked the box over to the Pope's bedside and gently placed it on top of the covers, near the bottom just beyond the Pope's feet. Then he undid the latch, but he made the mistake of inching the box door open somewhat. He was operating in the dark and wanted to be sure that it was open for the snake to get out, but as he eased the door open the snake struck and sunk its deadly fangs into the Monsignor's left hand.

He yelled and flipped his hand in an effort to get the snake off him before it could inject any venom into his system, but he was too late. He was paralyzed where he stood and dropped to the floor. He would be dead in a matter of minutes.

The commotion woke up the aged Martin who began to ask who was there, but the Death Adder struck again, this time sinking its fangs into the neck of the Pontiff. Since the venom entered

MURDER IN THE VATICAN

into the carotid artery the Pope didn't
have a chance to compete his sentence,
which began with "Who is ... ?" Those
were the last two words he ever spoke,
but he did let out a blood-curdling
scream, which roused the two guards at
the bedroom door.

They had let Secretary Corvi pass
in the Pope's sleeping quarters, because
he often went in and out to check on the
Pope and they assumed the box he was
carrying contained medication or
perhaps an atomizer.

When they rushed into the room
the lead guard flipped on the light and
saw the Pontiff writing in pain, still in
his bed. Next to the bed was the
Monsignor who was twitching, but less
so than the Pope.

MURDER IN THE VATICAN

The guard pressed forward to the beside and that's when the snake struck again, catching the guard on the forearm.

Quickly the second guard pulled out his sword and cut the Death Adder in two. The twin pieces fell to the floor, each convulsing like the other.

The first guard was holding his arm and yelling. He saw what the snake had apparently done to the Monsignor and the Pope and he was sure he was about to follow them into an agonizing death.

He didn't have to worry because the Death Adder had delivered all its venom into the two Prelates. He was just going to have a sore arm for his brave attempt to help his Pope.

CHAPTER THIRTY-TWO

There is a darkness in you. In all of us, probably. Beasts we keep chained. Ordinary men have to keep the chains strong, for if we let the beast loose then society will turn upon us with fiery vengeance. Kings though...well, who is there to turn upon them? So the chains are made of straw. It is the curse of kings, Helikaon, that they can become monsters. And they invariably do.
– David Gemmell, *Shield of Thunder*

The official story released to the Church membership and to the outside world was that Pope Martin VI died quietly in his sleep at the age of 87. As tradition dictated the death of the Pope was verified by the *Cardinal Camerlengo*, or the Vatican Chamberlain. This was done only after the *Cardinal Camerlengo* performed the rite of gently striking the head of the Pope with a small silver hammer while calling out his Christian

name three times. As there was no
response from Martin the *Cardinal
Camerlengo* declared him dead.

At that point the *Cardinal
Camerlengo* took possession of the Ring
of the Fisherman, which is worn by the
Pontiff and the Papal Seal.

This began the *Sede Vacante*, the
Empty Seat, of the leader of the Holy
Roman Church. After the details of the
Pope's burial were attended to, the
Vatican Cardinals moved to convene a
meeting of the College of Cardinals to
elect a new Pope, also known as The
Bishop of Rome, the apostolic successor
of Saint Peter and the earthly head of
the Roman Catholic Church.

The Papal Conclave has been the
electoral institution at the Vatican for
nearly a millennium and that following
the death of Pope Martin was not the

MURDER IN THE VATICAN

first one to be held because of the murder of the Pontiff.

Before the Cardinals who would elect the new Pope convened, they had to observe a variety of rituals.

The Cardinals were required to listen to two sermons before the election. The first they heard before actually entering the Papal Conclave; the second one they heard once they were inside the Sistine Chapel.

On the day designated by the Congregations of the Cardinals, the Cardinal Electors assembled in St. Peter's Basilica to celebrate the Eucharist. Then they made their way to the Pauline Chapel of the Palace of the Vatican. From there they moved in procession while singing traditional songs. Then they took the set oath:

MURDER IN THE VATICAN

*Et ego, (first name), Cardinalis
(surname), spondeo, voveo, ac iuro. Sic
me Deus adiuvet et haec Sancta Dei
Evangelia, quae manu mea tango.*
In English this translated: And I (name),
Cardinal (last name), promise, vow and
swear. Thus, may god help me and
these Holy Gospels, which I touch with
my hand.

Once all the Cardinals had
completed swearing the oath, the
Master of the Papal Liturgical
Celebrations ordered all individuals
other than the Cardinal Electors out of
the Sistine Chapel by saying, "*Extra
omnes!*" He then locked the doors and
the Cardinal Electors stayed inside for
the first day's balloting.

The election of the new Pope took
four days, the first three indicating to
the world outside that no agreement

had been reached by the color of the
smoke from the burning of the ballots. If
a two-thirds majority cannot be reached
the chimney smoke is black or *fumata
nera*.

On the fourth day the smoke was
fumata bianca – white, signaling the
election of a new Pontiff.

Cardinal Giovani Donati had done
some intense politicking among the
electors and, consequently, ascended to
the Throne of St. Peter.

Once it was clear from the
balloting the Donati was to be the next
Pope, the Cardinal Dean summoned the
Secretary of the College of Cardinals and
the Master of Papal Liturgical
Celebrations into the hall. In the
presence of all the Cardinals the
Cardinal Dean asked the Pope-elect if he
assented to becoming Pontiff using the

MURDER IN THE VATICAN

Latin phrase, "*Acceptasne electionem de te canonice factam in Summum Pontificem?*"

Cardinal Donati responded in Latin, "*Accipio.*" He was then dressed in the Pontifical Robes and the Ring of the Fisherman was placed on his finger. He was then led by two Cardinals to the balcony and gave his blessing to the cheering throng below in St. Peter's Square.

MURDER IN THE VATICAN

CHAPTER THIRTY-THREE

Just because something isn't a lie does not mean that it isn't deceptive. A liar knows that he is a liar, but one who speaks mere portions of truth in order to deceive is a craftsman of destruction.
— Criss Jami, Writer

It wasn't a week before the new Pope, the former Cardinal Donati, now Pope Pius XIII, came out in support of the newly installed administration of Prime Minister Servio Ganza. Going beyond the restraint of most Popes' comments on politics, Pope Pius strongly supported the New Fascism, as the newspapers were calling Ganza's policies.

Like the Prime Minister himself, Pope Pius justified establishing a totalitarian government in Italy to fight the ISIS threat. He lauded Mussolini for

MURDER IN THE VATICAN

enabling the establishment of a Vatican State, called both him and Ganza true Christians and went on to bemoan the early downfall of Mussolini, which according to Pope Pius, was due to foul play on the part of the invading Allied Powers.

"Look where the democracy of the Allies has gotten the world," he spewed. "The world is in a mess and that would not have been the case if Fascism and Nazism had prevailed."

Much of the press in the western countries came out against both the ideological comments of both Prime Minister Ganza and Pope Pius XIII. In fact, many in the Catholic Church were aghast at the Pope's comments. Clergy everywhere gave sermons denouncing the remarks of the new Pope. On a wider scale, people within democratic countries were in shock and expressed their outrage at such outlandish political commentaries.

Within the Vatican too, Prelates were mostly horrified at the political nature of the Pope's speech. This was especially true of Cardinal Nazario Viola, who had not only *not* voted for Donati, but who had, behind the scenes during the Papal Conclave, actively promoted another Cardinal; or as he put it to his fellow electors, "Anyone but Donati."

On the lighter side, in the valet network, it was said that outside the Vatican there was a new *Il Duce* and also inside. Some in private even took to calling the new Pontiff "Pope Mussolini." Others shortened it to *"Papa Duce."*

Obviously Stone Harrison was upset with the result of the Papal Conclave. One of the first things Pope

MURDER IN THE VATICAN

Pius did was to eject Stone from his Vatican digs and cancel the investigation started by his predecessor.

Not unhappily, Stone moved in with Fabiola. They both saw it as a temporary situation because her flat was very small, but they had decided to look for a bigger one when things settled down. Stone was not give up on the investigation.

Things were anything but settled when Marty Murphy showed up at Fabiola's apartment with news of the second ISIS bomber, or at least the man he suspected to be in Rome to bomb the Vatican.

"His name is Mamoun Khauli and he is in room 442 at the *Gran Meliá Rome Hotel.*"

"Why do you think he is the bomber?" Stone asked.

MURDER IN THE VATICAN

"I bribed one of the maids who cleans his room. She alerted me when he went out and I searched through his things. You know what I found?"

"Let me guess," said Fabiola jumping in, "a suicide vest."

"Stuffed with plastic explosive clay and lots of ball bearings, nuts and bolts – stuff to do damage to anyone unlucky enough to be standing nearby when he sets the goddamned thing off."

Fabiola was making some tea in the flat's open efficiency kitchen and moaned, "Now we have a monster for a Pope and a monster who wants to blow him to Kingdom Come."

Caustically Stone said, "It wouldn't be so bad if the bomber only got to Donati, but it's the hundreds around him I'm concerned about."

MURDER IN THE VATICAN

"We can't just take the guy out, can we?" asked Marty Murphy.

Stone slammed his fist on the table, "I'm not being paid by the Vatican anymore, but I'll be damned if I'm going to give up on nailing Donati, Pope or no Pope and no way am I going to allow an ISIS bomber to complete his suicidal mission."

Fabiola set three cups of Tetley's Tea on the table and admonished Stone not to pound the table again. Then she asked Marty, "Where is the bomber now? He doesn't have the vest with him I hope."

"I don't know where he went, but I made sure the vest was still in his room."

Stone took a sip of his tea and did the "Ummm good" thing for Fabiola. Then he said, "When our little tea time is over we had better head over to the hotel and pay Mr. Khauli a visit."

"He's probably there now," assured Marty Murphy. "The maid says he sleeps in the afternoon and goes out partying at night. She knows this because he came home so drunk one night that he couldn't get into his room and the night clerk had to open the room for him."

Fabiola said, "Muslims aren't supposed to drink alcohol, but these suicide bombers are given a special license to break the rules."

"And like James Bond, a license to kill."

****

Fabiola, Stone & Marty were standing in front of the room of Mamoun Khauli – room 442 at the *Gran Meliá*

MURDER IN THE VATICAN

Rome Hotel. Murphy knocked and said, "Message for Mamoun Khauli."

There was a stirring inside and then the door opened. Mamoun Khauli looked at the three individuals who were not dressed like bellhops and surprise crawled across his face, followed by confusion and then fear.

"Mamoun, we would like a word with you," said Stone with his hand on his pocketed pistol.

"Who are you?" asked Khauli, stepped back. "How do you know my name?"

The three entered the room and Stone continued in a soothing voice. He didn't want this young man going for a gun or, worse yet, the explosive vest. "We would like to talk to you about the bombing." Stone really didn't know how to start, so he tried the direct approach.

352

MURDER IN THE VATICAN

Instinctively Khauli's eyes went to the closet, but Murphy had positioned himself in front of it. He said, "We know you have a suicide vest."

Panic spread over the young Syrian. His right eye began to twitch wildly.

"We don't want to hurt you," said Fabiola, trying the motherly approach. "We would like to talk you out of killing innocent people though."

Mamoun Khauli stumbled back against his bed and sat down heavily, "I ... I ... aghh ... ." He put his face in his hands and began to whimper.

Fabiola interrupted, "We would like you to tell us how you came to this point." She sat next to Mamoun Khauli on the bed and put her arm around him. His shoulders slumped and the tension seemed to go out of his body. The whimpering turned to crying.

Then, wiping his eyes, Khauli slowly told his story. All of them had read versions of it in newspapers with regard to other bombers and Fabiola had even written some of the articles. But it was when Khauli got to the present that it began to change, "I ... I have been trying to think of a way to get out of this. I don't want to die and I don't want to kill anyone."

"We are here to help you accomplish that," said Fabiola, soothingly.

"But if I don't do it they will kill my mother and father – my whole family. If I do it they get paid by the Caliph. He promised me."

Stone spoke in an authoritative voice, "Not if we stage your death in a way that it appears that you had tried to set off the vest, but that you were shot and killed before that."

Mamoun Khauli tried to absorb this. After a moment he asked, "And then what? I could never go back to Syria."

"We have friends who can give you a new life in America or somewhere in Europe. You can live a normal life, worship as a Muslim and find a wife and have children like everybody else not caught in the ISIS web."

Mamoun Khauli hung his head and tried hard to absorb this.

Marty Murphy opened the closet and gently removed the explosive-laden vest. It looked both lethal and evil at the same time. Murphy removed a pillowcase and dropped the vest in.

Then he asked, "Do you have any more weapons or explosives?"

Khauli nodded, got up and opened the drawer of his bedside table. He began to reach in, but Stone was right behind him, "Let me get that," he said in the same deep commanding voice.

Harrison removed the pistol and asked, "Any more?"

Khauli shook his head, "No. The Caliph wanted me to blow people up, not shoot them. I don't even have any extra bullets for it."

Stone emptied the gun of its bullets then pulled out his mobile phone and dialed a number. When the other party answered, Stone said, "You can come up now."

Within two minutes Gustav Holtz of the *Pan-European Anti-Terrorism Task Force* came through the open door. Two

MURDER IN THE VATICAN

PEATTF officers stayed in the hallway, guarding the door.

Stone explained to Holtz that the young man had had a change of heart. Holtz went over to Mamoun Khauli and patted him on the shoulder. "Good boy. We can give you a whole new life."

Then Khauli opened up and explained that he had been really confused by the news of the killings at the parliament building in Rome. "Those were not ISIS men. I asked the Caliph about that and he said that ISIS was going to take credit for it in a video, but that someone had been impersonating ISIS fighters."

"It is nice to hear that from you," said the head of *PEATTF*. "That jibes with our information. Somebody wanted that to look like Islamic terrorism."

MURDER IN THE VATICAN

Fabiola said softly, "And it was Fascist terrorism."

****

It took some doing to get a crowd together outside of St. Peter's Basilica, but when the *PEATTF* officers explained that they would be in a movie they had more tourists on their hands than they needed.

In the carefully orchestrated film Mamoun Khauli was seen mingling in the crowd. He wore a bulky coat, which he threw open exposing a vest, although one without explosives. Then he shouted, "*Allah a akbar*," and started to press the button on his vest, but shots rang out and armed *PEATTF* officers appeared and fired several more shots into the jerking body of Mamoun Khauli in his first staring film role.

MURDER IN THE VATICAN

The officers were firing blanks and the vest Khauli was wearing was a Kevlar vest designed to prevent any harm to him from the packing wads fired from the blanks.

Neither Stone nor Fabiola ever knew what happened to the young man, but Holtz assured them that Mamoun Khauli was on a plane to America shortly after they unceremoniously dragged his "bullet riddled corpse" away in the final scene of the little movie that made its way into ISIS hands in faraway Syria. It was never going to win an Oscar, but it did the trick.

MURDER IN THE VATICAN

CHAPTER THIRTY-FOUR

The monkish vows keep us far from that sink of vice that is the female body, but often they bring us close to other errors. Can I finally hide from myself the fact that even today my old age is still stirred by the noonday demon when my eyes, in choir, happen to linger on the beardless face of a novice, pure and fresh as a maiden's?
— Umberto Eco, *The Name of the Rose*

With the bombing threat out of the way Stone Harrison returned to his pursuit of evidence on Vatican shenanigans. He decided to follow up on the *Propaganda Due* angle.

"What do you know about these Bunga Bunga parties?" Stone asked Fabiola.

"*La Dolce Vita* type merrymaking, from what I've heard."

"Yeah, me too."

"Why?"

MURDER IN THE VATICAN

"I know that Lippi is tight with Donati and Sadowski. All I have is smoke and I need fire – real, hard evidence of wrongdoing by those two. Where does Lippi hold those shindigs?

"He's got a villa on Lake Lugano near the village of San Mamete."

"Fancy a drive?"

"To Lake Lugano?"

"Smart gal."

"And this smart gal likes drives outside of Rome. The Italian countryside is gorgeous at almost any time of year, but in the springtime like this – beyond beautiful."

****

As Harrison maneuvered the rental car through the tiny village of San Mamete Fabiola asked him, "What are we going to do when we get there? Lippi is probably in Rome.

MURDER IN THE VATICAN

"That's exactly what I'm counting on."

"So you're going to break into his place?"

"In a manner of speaking."

"Well since I'm your partner in crime, how about *speaking* your ideas to me."

"You'll see."

"Great. Men are such great conversationalists."

"That's sarcasm, right?"

"Yeah, the dripping version of sarcasm."

"An Italian specialty, I assume."

"Yeah, like *Pasta Fazoli.*"

"I like *Pasta al Burro con Formaggino* better."

"You weren't meant to like the sarcasm Buster Brown."

MURDER IN THE VATICAN

"Buster Brown was an early 20th century comic strip character."

"My point exactly," said Fabiola, with a degree of self-satisfaction.

The repartee ended there because Stone pulled into the graveled arc of a driveway in front of Lippi's getaway villa.

As he got out of the car he said, "Follow my lead."

He rang the doorbell and it was answered by a uniformed maid, "*Sì?*"

In his broken Italian Stone explained that they were supposed to meet *Signore* Lippi.

Fabiola caught his drift and asked, *È di mister Lippi ancora qui?*"

The maid said that he hadn't arrived yet, but let them in, telling them to wait by the pool. She would fetch them drinks. "*E 'la birra va bene?*"

MURDER IN THE VATICAN

"Yes, beer will be fine," agreed Stone.

When they were on the patio and drinking their Peroni beers Fabiola asked, "What now? I am assuming Lippi is not coming. What's the plan?"

"When I finish my beer I'm going to ask to use the bathroom. I want to have as much time as possible to explore, so I'll leave it up to you how to keep the maid away from me."

The reporter decided to go with her strength. She told the maid that she was a newspaper reporter for *Il Messaggero* in Rome. "I'm doing a long piece on various kinds of work people do. Could you sit for a while so that I can interview you?" she asked the maid.

While the faux interview was in play Stone poked around what appeared to be Lippi's office. In the course of his snooping he noticed a door to what seemed to be a closet. He opened it and found himself looking at shelves of videotapes, each one labeled with a man's name.

They were in alphabetical order and Stone immediately went to the Ds and found Donati.

"Bingo for Bunga Bunga," he said aloud.

He put the tape in his pocket and looked for Sadowski, but there was no tape labeled with that name, although there were various others in the S category.

Stone looked around as long as he thought he could appear to be at the bathroom and then returned to the poolside patio to find Fabiola acting in her reporter role.

MURDER IN THE VATICAN

Stone announced that he had just received a call from *Signore* Lippi and that he had been detained in Rome. "He wants us to hurry back love. We are to meet him at the *Propaganda Due* lodge."

Fabiola thanked the maid for the beer and the interview and they beat a hasty retreat to the car.

****

Back at the apartment Stone put the videotape into Fabiola's player and they sat back to watch. They were shocked at what they saw. The tape showed Cardinal Donati naked and having anal intercourse with a young boy.

"This is dynamite stuff," said Fabiola in the understatement of the year.

MURDER IN THE VATICAN

"This is the man who became Pope. Do you realize what we have here?"

"I already said dynamite. That means its explosive."

"And then some," added the detective.

"What are you going to do with it?" asked Fabiola.

"We obtained it illegally, so it won't be of much use in a court of law, but given Donati's position now I don't think we need to worry about the niceties of a trail."

"You're not thinking of going public with it, are you?"

"Not unless Plan A doesn't work."

"And what is Plan A?"

"We copy it, put this one in a safe deposit box, leave the key and instructions with a lawyer in case something bad happens to us and then confront the Pope with it. He'll have the option to resign as Pontiff or face the very bad press that would result in the public getting to see this."

"He may use his power to try to come after us. He already doesn't like you," said Fabiola.

"That's why we put our insurance with the lawyer and the second tape. We make sure Donati understands what will happen if he fights us."

Fabiola was silent for a while and then said, "I think it's a good plan. Let's do it."

"I thought you might want an exclusive on this story. Exposing a sitting Pope of pedophilia with video evidence would sure be a feather in your newspaper hat."

MURDER IN THE VATICAN

"There is not such thing as a newspaper hat."

"If you broke this story for your newspaper the editor would give you one. They'd give me a lot more than a hat, but no – we go with Plan A."

"Good girl."

Fabiola faked a 'hurt little girl' pose and said, "I thought you liked me being the bad girl."

Stone laughed, "That's another thing sweetheart."

"When do we get to do that 'other thing'?"

"As soon as we bring down the most powerful man in the religious world."

MURDER IN THE VATICAN

CHAPTER THIRTY-FIVE

The known martyrs – those who actually,
voluntarily sought death and rejoiced in the fact –
had been the kamikaze pilots, immolating
themselves to propitiate a 'divine' emperor who
looked (as Orwell once phrased it) like a monkey
on a stick. Their Christian predecessors had
endured torture and death (as well as inflicted it) in
order to set up a theocracy. Their modern
equivalents would be the suicide murderers, who
mostly have the same aim in mind. About people
who set out to lose their lives, then, there seems to
hang an air of fanaticism: a gigantic sense of self-
importance unattractively fused with a masochistic
tendency to self-abnegation.
— Christopher Hitchens, *Hitch-22: A Memoir*

Caliph Abu Bakr al Baghdadi was
outraged at the establishment of a
fascist regime in Italy, but he was even
more incensed by the fact that the
authorities found and killed the second
bomber at the Vatican. He was unaware
that the video broadcast of the killing of

the young Syrian bomber was faked by Interpol and Mamoun Khauli was immediately whisked off to a new life in the United States.

"I want to strike at the heart of Italy," said Caliph Abu Bakr al Baghdadi. "We must not let a temporary setback appear as defeat in the eyes of the world."

"We have many bombers at our disposal," said Ahlam Waheeb, coldly. He was a trusted lieutenant of the Caliph and a man known as a killer unencumbered by a conscience. As a true believer in the warped version of Islam that ISIS was putting forth, Ahlam Waheeb's world was black and white. There were no moral gray areas. There was no sympathy for infidels or Muslims of a different persuasion. ISIS was right and the world was wrong. Simple as that.

"I've been giving this a lot of thought," said the ISIS boss, "we need to make a big splash in the middle of the heart of Italy."

"The Vatican again?" asked Ahlam Waheeb.

"No, we did that. Anyway the new Pope has had dealings with us. He is compromised by that. We can use him in the future. Now we strike the secular arm of that infidel state. We kill the new Prime Minister and whoever else in his administration happens to be near our martyr when he presses the button."

"How do we get brother close to the Prime Minister? Those men are closely guarded."

"There are always cracks in any piece of armor."

MURDER IN THE VATICAN

Ahlam Waheeb sat up straight, "That's a pithy statement. Who said that?"

"Lao-Tzu."

"Who is he?" asked Ahlam Waheeb, disingenuously.

"*Was.* He is long since dead. He wrote *The Art of Warfare.*"

Actually Ahlam Waheeb knew that his leader was wrong in attributing *The Art of Warfare* to Lao-Tzu. He wouldn't say so, but he knew that Lao-Tzu was the founder of Taoism, a philosophy antithetical to Islam and the ISIS point of view.

The lieutenant knew that *Master Sun's Rules of Warfare* was written by the 5th century philosopher Sun Wu. Sometimes lieutenants need to keep their mouths shut in the presence of generals. This was one of those times.

MURDER IN THE VATICAN

"So what are the cracks in the armor we can exploit?"

"That is your job. I'm putting you in charge of the operation in Rome. Get back to me when you have a plan."

"I will do so, Caliph. And we will be successful, *Insha'Allah*."

"Yes, always *Insha'Allah*."

****

Prime Minister Servio Ganza was enjoying his move out of the realm of Underworld criminality to the world of political criminality. He liked his new office and most of all he liked the fact that he could give press conferences and all the media came. He liked seeing himself on television. He made a point to be a very visible public servant, although he thought of himself more as a strong leader, not in any way a servant of the people.

MURDER IN THE VATICAN

In Ganza's mind the people should blindly follow a strong leader. He had been successful as a *capo forte* and now he would be equally effective as a *duce forte*.

This was the chink in Ganza's armor that Ahlam Waheeb felt would be his undoing.

It was on the steps of the *Palazzo Chigi*, the office building of the Italian Prime Minister, that Ganza positioned himself behind the makeshift podium to deliver his 14th "Message to the Nation."

The new Mussolini tapped the microphone to see if it was working and smiled down at the gaggle of reporters and cameras beneath him. He didn't have to tap the mic because now he had a cadre of professional technicians to make sure the sound system worked

MURDER IN THE VATICAN

properly before it was to be used. He did anyway, out of habit.

The lower steps were covered with media types and some interested spectators. One interested spectator was Osama al-Wuhayshi. He was wearing an explosive vest with nearly enough dynamite to melt the steps of the *Palazzo Chigi*.

That was an exaggeration. A dynamite blast, no matter how strong, could not melt concrete. What it did do when al-Wuhayshi pressed the button was knock the head off the statue of Marcus Aurelius in the *Piazza Colonna* across the street. When the marble head crashed down it hit a homeless man who was leaning against the column and just tipping his wine bottle to his lips. Most people who knew the man before he became a bum had

MURDER IN THE VATICAN

thought he would die of alcohol. Instead he died of a falling bust. Death by marble.

Closer to the blast several people also lost their heads like the image of the Roman Emperor, but in addition to decapitation the explosion took away their arms, legs, faces and much of their torsos.

The former Mafioso, though he had not formally relinquished that Underworld label, was also turned to hamburger and spread among the bits and pieces of the other victims of the bombing.

Standing slightly behind Servio Ganza when the bomb was detonated was the General of the Army, LLario Forcella, who had recently been given the supplementary title of Deputy Prime Minister. He, along with many in the

MURDER IN THE VATICAN

new fascist regime, was blown into
minced oblivion.

MURDER IN THE VATICAN

CHAPTER THIRTY-SIX

Now since shame is a mental picture of disgrace, in which we shrink from the disgrace itself and not from its consequences, and we only care what opinion is held of us because of the people who form that opinion, it follows that the people before whom we feel shame are those whose opinion of us matters to us.
— Aristotle, *The Rhetoric & The Poetics of Aristotle*

The assassination of Prime Minister Servio Ganza and many of his cabinet shocked the nation. Pope Pius XIII was also shocked, but not as much by the suicide bombing of his friend, but by the visit of Stone Harrison and the revelation that he had been secretly videotaped at the Bunga Bunga parties fucking young boys.

Stone knew that Donati would not admit him to his Vatican chambers, so he got Captain Celso Palmisano to get

four of the Pontifical Swiss Guards to
usher him and the Captain of the
Gendarmeria into the presence of Pope
Pius XIII while he was dining with Paul
Sadowski, a Bishop he had recently
promoted to Cardinal.

The Swiss Guards had been
handpicked by Palmisano because of
their fierce commitment to Catholic
orthodoxy. He played the tape for them
and explained that they needed to have
the Pope see it so that he could resign
and let a more sinless man move on to
the Throne of St. Peter.

The Swiss Guards physically
picked up Donati by the arms and
hustled him into his Papal apartment.
Once inside they forced him to sit before
his television and Stone put the video
into the player.

MURDER IN THE VATICAN

Donati tried to protest, saying that it was not him on the screen, that the tape had been doctored; but it was to no avail because all present knew he was lying, even the four Swiss Guards, one of whom had to rush into the Pontiff's bathroom to vomit after seeing the obscene acts.

Perhaps consensual sex with a woman may have been acceptable, but these were young boys who were handcuffed to the bed, raped and beaten.

Pope Pius had no defense. When Stone Harrison and the others left him he was sitting slouched in his chair. His head was hanging down in total dejection.

On their way out of the papal quarters Palmisano and Harrison ran into Sadowski, who had remained at the dining room table finishing his Peking Duck with Hoisin sauce.

Captain Palmisano walked up to the Cardinal and slapped him hard across the cheek. "You shithead," shouted Palmisano, "we know that you've been using the Vatican Bank for illicit purposes. This detective has hard evidence to the fact that you have been laundering money for the Roman Mafia and even ISIS, for God's sake."

Sadowski tried to protest, neither Stone nor Celso Palmisano were having any of it.

"Here's what you are going to do. Tomorrow morning at the latest you will submit your resignation as Director of the Vatican Bank. As head of the Vatican's *Gendarmeria* I'm going to place the bank in a receivership until an honest Director can be found. What you do with the rest of your miserable life is up to you."

Celso Palmisano was saying this while backed up by four Swiss Guards wearing their medieval helmets with the red plumage, their blue-yellow-red stripped uniforms and holding nine-foot half–pike spears.

Paul Sadowski began to whimper. An era of malfeasance had ended over Peking Duck with Hoisin sauce.

****

All of Italy, and especially those in Rome, were still reeling from the bombing that brought down Ganza's government when two more shockwaves hit, both coming less than a week after the bombing at the *Palazzo Chigi*.

The first surprise was a Vatican announcement that Pope Pius XIII, after

MURDER IN THE VATICAN

less than a month on the Throne of St. Peter, had suffered a massive heart attack.

The truth, known to only a few Vatican insiders and the outsiders Stone Harrison and Fabiola Bellandi, was that the disgraced Pontiff had sliced his wrists and bled to death. His pale naked body was found naked in the papal bathtub.

The second blow to the sensibilities of the general public was the suicide of Cardinal Paul Sadowski, Head of the Vatican Bank. The powerful Cardinals of the Vatican did not even try to hide the fact that Sadowski had shot himself through the roof of his mouth. Apparently he had not been liked for years and it was felt that announcing his suicide would provide him with more time in purgatory trying to make up for his earthly sins.

Some, however, thought that Paul Sadowski, as a suicide, would have gone directly to Hell to burn forever.

Either way, his valet spent hours trying to clean his brains, skull and hair off the bathroom ceiling.

MURDER IN THE VATICAN

CHAPTER THIRTY-SEVEN

Reshaping life! People who can say that have never understood a thing about life – they have never felt its breath, its heartbeat – however much they have seen or done. They look on it as a lump of raw material that needs to be processed by them, to be ennobled by their touch. But life is never a material, a substance to be molded. If you want to know, life is the principle of self-renewal, it is constantly renewing and remaking and changing and transfiguring itself, it is infinitely beyond your or my obtuse theories about it.
— Boris Pasternak, *Doctor Zhivago*

Italy has been through a lot over the centuries – the sacking of Rome by the Visigoths in 410, then in 455 more destruction by the Vandals. Rome was not done. Again in 546 it was sacked by King Totila of the Goths. Yet again in 846 the Saracens got their turn. It wasn't until 1084 that the Christian crusaders under the Norman Robert

MURDER IN THE VATICAN

Guiscard performed yet another devastation. Finally in 1527 the City of Seven Hills again got sacked by the mutinous troops of the Holy Roman Emperor, Charles V.

Mama Italia always seemed to bounce back, to regenerate Her vitality and move forward.

She did it again after the death of two Prime Ministers and two Popes within weeks of each other. Italians still took four-hour lunch breaks and a month off in August to bake themselves on sandy beaches in the Mediterranean or North Africa. Chefs made pasta. Cardinal Nazario Viola was installed as Pope Gregory XVII and was busy cleaning house at the Vatican. Occasionally an Italian man with too

MURDER IN THE VATICAN

much testosterone and not enough
couth would pinch a girl's butt on the

metro, on the street, in a movie house –
well, you get the picture. Italy was
bouncing back to normality.

Stone and Fabiola had to find their
normality. She was Italian with a fine
job as a reporter at a main newspaper.
He was a tenured professor at the best
university in Europe.

They wanted to stay together, but
it was a quandary as to where they
should reside. And both of them being
rather on the intelligent side, they came
up with a parsimonious solution. Stone
would apply to the University of Rome
for a job and Fabiola would apply for a
position as a reporter on *The Cambridge*

MURDER IN THE VATICAN

Evening News, the most read newspaper in Cambridgeshire.

Their pact said that whichever one of them got a job offer would decide where they would reside.

The problem was that both of them were offered employment.

So they put their intelligence aside and flipped a coin. Cambridge won and *The Cambridge Evening News* got a fiery Italian on its staff.

The couple bought a house on Mulberry Close, but as the children came along over the years they had to move to a bigger house and bought one from a Cambridge professor on Adams Road.

Stone continued with his writing at Emmanuel College and published several books in his subject area and Fabiola, besides becoming Assistant

MURDER IN THE VATICAN

Editor of *The Cambridge Evening News*, having two wonderful children, a boy and a girl, also published a book.

It was a murder mystery based in the Vatican.

THE END

To contact the author email him at docelm42@gmail.com

Printed in Great Britain
by Amazon

27349680R00218